First published in the UK by HarperCollins Children's Books in 2009

1 3 5 7 9 10 8 6 4 2

ISBN 13: 978-0-00-729890-7

Licensed by:

Prime Suspect

by Richard Dungworth

HarperCollins *Children's Books*

You've just got off the hover-tram from school, and are waiting to take the pedestrian travelator across the busy skyway that runs past the block where you live.

Robot-piloted freight trucks thunder past, carrying anything and everything that the citizens of 22nd century Detroit need in a hurry.

The travelator suddenly purrs into motion. An electronic voice asks you to 'Please cross now – and have a nice day!'

You step on, without even bothering to check the traffic – you know that once the crossing is activated, any oncoming trucks will be automatically brought to a halt.

At least, that's what *should* happen.

But as you reach the middle of the skyway, a massive truck comes rumbling towards you, showing no sign of slowing.

The next few seconds seem to pass in slow motion. As you freeze, terrified, in the path of the fast-approaching truck, you hear the roar of another engine. A second vehicle is bearing down upon you from the opposite direction – a large red and blue fire truck.

The fire truck suddenly explodes into a mass of mechanical parts, which swiftly recombine –

separating, spinning, interlocking. Within moments, the vehicle has changed into an entirely different entity – a colossal, ten metre tall robot, bearing a gigantic axe.

The robot sprints towards you, sweeps you up in one massive metal hand, then plants the end of his axe's long shaft on the skyway and launches himself into the air. You soar, pole-vault style, up and over the oncoming freight truck. It rushes beneath you, missing you by centimetres.

Your metal saviour lands lightly beside the skyway, carefully releases you, then spins to launch a grapple line from one arm. The grapple attaches itself to the runaway truck's motor unit. As the line jerks taut, the unit is torn away, bringing the truck to a standstill.

The giant robot swiftly retracts his grapple line, then crouches in front of you.

'The vehicle's auto-regulator must have malfunctioned.'

His synthetic voice is deep and resonating.

'Did you sustain any damage?'

You shake your head, speechless.

The robot smiles warmly.

'My sensors detect a degree of system shock. I will escort you home.' He dips his massive metal head.

'Optimus Prime, formerly of the Cybertronian Autobot Academy, at your service!'

As your brain finally restarts, you wonder whether arriving home with a giant alien robot might freak your mum out more than a little…

To accept Prime's offer, turn to 26.
To say 'Thanks, but I'm OK,' turn to 17.

After a frantic search, you find another exit. You and your two robotic companions hastily escape the building, and hurry away.

You haven't gone far when a hulking green metallic giant – another Autobot – comes thudding towards you.

'Bulkhead!' exclaims Prowl. 'What kept you?'

'Sorry guys.' The colossal stranger looks a little embarrassed. 'I was… erm… at an outdoor laser-sculpture exhibition across town when I got the boss's signal.'

'Ever the artist!' mocks Prowl. 'Well – we'd best catch up with Optimus.' He closes his eyes for a few moments in concentration. 'Fortunately, my high resolution senses can still just about pick up his trail.'

In a rapid, fluid metamorphosis, Prowl changes into a sleek gold and black motorcycle. He pulls in front of you, engine purring.

'You better get on,' drawls Prowl's voice. 'But mind the chrome.'

A short – but memorable – high-speed ride later, you find yourself outside the main building of a sprawling research complex, in the company of Sari and her five Autobot friends. Prime is looming over a man in a grey security guard uniform, who is talking to him rather nervously.

To ask Sari what's going on, turn to 83.
To talk with Prime, turn to 52.

Once on the building's upper level, you quickly find somewhere to lie low. It looks like you've evaded your pursuers – until a pair of police officers with sniffer dog-bots slowly approach. The robotic dogs have obviously picked up your scent, though the officers have yet to spot you.

Before they do, a large robotic figure drops from nowhere to land lightly just in front of them. He is black and gold, a little taller than Bumblebee, and sleekly built.

'It's Prowl!' hisses Bumblebee.

The black Autobot gives the surprised officers a wry smile, then sprints past them in the opposite direction to where you are hiding. After a moment's hesitation, the officers and their dog-bots give chase.

'Well, I think that worked rather well, don't you?' drawls a voice just behind you. You do a double-take as a robot identical to the one you've just watched run off steps from the shadows.

Bumblebee grins at him. 'The old hologram decoy, eh? Neat.'

'Illusion is often more effective than brute force,' observes Prowl.

'Uh-huh,' says Bumblebee, sounding

unconvinced. 'Anyhow – I need to check on how Optimus is getting on. You sit tight with these two.'

As Bumblebee hurries away, Prowl looks a bit put out.

'Marvellous. Ah, well – I suggest we use this time for spiritual self-improvement. A little Circuit-Su meditation will be just the thing…'

He adopts a crossed-legged sitting posture, closes his eyes, and falls silent.

To ask Sari what 'Circuit-Su' is, turn to 81.

To try a little meditation yourself, turn to 58.

Your resistance is futile – however hard you struggle, you cannot get free.

Then, to your great relief, the real Prime arrives on the scene. Taking in your predicament in a split second, he draws his mighty axe and sends it hurtling towards his impostor.

Your captor is forced to release you as he reacts to Prime's attack. He sidesteps the axe, turns, and sprints away. As Prime gives chase, you and Sari race after him.

The pursuit leads to the largest warehouse chamber you have yet seen. Inside, thousands of Pixie-6 'bots stand in neat rows, individually packaged in transparent capsules.

A central platform, supported by a tall, thin pedestal, overlooks the entire area. Prime's impostor hurries towards it, launches a line-grapple at the platform's underside, and rapidly hauls himself up.

'Whoever you are,' booms Prime, as his clone mounts the platform, 'you cannot escape. My Autobot comrades are close by.'

'Escape! Why should I want to escape?' scoffs the impostor. 'Let your puny friends come – *I* have an *army* at my command!'

He lifts a small black sphere above his head. As he focuses his deranged stare on it, the Pixie-6 'bots suddenly come to life, each one bursting from its packaging.

'This is what I broke into the *HomeTech* labs for! With my modifications, this control sphere gives me command of not just one, but all these delightful little machines!'

As the Pixie-6s trundle your way, each extends a small probe from its casing.

'And their effectiveness when used in collaboration is most surprising. Take their anti-pest phasers, for instance…'

Each Pixie-6 probe suddenly emits a tiny energy beam. The thousands of beams converge to form a single crackling strand of energy, which leaps at Prime's chest like lightening. He slumps to the floor.

'Imagine my little pets in every human household!' cackles the impostor. 'And by appearing as Prime, I have ensured that his precious humans will blame him for the chaos I shall wreak!'

You see Prime stirring. If you can keep his impostor talking, he might have time to recover.

To compliment the impostor on his cunning, turn to 19.
To ask him who he *really* is, turn to 53.

You follow the tracking signal south until you join the Detroit river several kilometres out of the city. Prowl pulls up beside the other Autobot vehicles at the river's edge.

The river is very wide here. At its centre floats a huge, white, cubic structure, like a colossal sugar-lump. There is a large opening in its downstream face, around which several hover-freighters are moored.

You dismount. The four Autobots adopt robot form.

'They call it the WaterShed,' says Prime, gesturing to the floating structure. 'It's a giant warehouse. *HomeTech* store their finished 'bots in it. And according to our signal, our felon is somewhere inside.'

He raises a massive metal arm, and launches his rocket-powered grapple over the fifty metre channel of water separating you from the floating building. It lodges in a service gantry on its near side.

Prime holds the line high and taut.

'OK, Prowl. Show them how it's done.'

A burst from Prowl's rocket boots enables him to grasp the line. Hanging from it, he begins to monkey-swing his way over the open water.

Bulkhead squats down with his back to you and Sari.

'Guess you two will be needing a ride! Jump on!'

Minutes later, after a stomach-churning piggyback trip along the grapple line, you are standing beside Bumblebee, Prowl and Bulkhead on the gantry. You watch as Prime retracts the line, propelling himself across the water like a giant water skier, before being pulled up to join you.

'Now we're all aboard,' says Bulkhead. 'Let's take a look around.'

He peels back a large section of the Watershed's thick alloy skin. Prime leads the way inside – into a wide passageway lined with stacks of white cargo containers.

To examine the containers, turn to 61.
To follow the passageway, turn to 37.

You narrowly dodge Blitzwing's fiery attack. As he prepares to launch another, Prime snatches up both you and Sari in his massive metal hands.

'I cannot protect you here! We need to move out!'

He sprints away, with your flame-throwing enemy in hot – very hot – pursuit.

Your flight brings you to a vast warehouse chamber, lined with hundreds of vertical transparent tubes. Pixie-6 helpbots – thousands in total – are stacked inside each tube.

'They're pneumatic chutes,' yells Sari to you. 'Dad uses them to pick-and-pack 'bots in the Sumdac warehouses.'

Prime puts you down near the chutes, then turns to face Blitzwing, who by now has joined you.

The Decepticon takes out the small sphere once more. He summons a rising column of flame beneath it, lifting it high into the air.

As he fixes his fiery gaze on the sphere above, the Pixie-6 'bots come alive. Streaming from the chute openings, they fall into ranks beside Blitzwing.

'With my modifications, the control sphere gives me remote command of every one of *HomeTech*'s precious 'bots!' rants the Decepticon. 'My own private robot army!'

Each Pixie-6 suddenly deploys one or more of its domestic tools – from laser-drills to slicing-wheels – in a threatening fashion.

'And thanks to my holotech disguise as your pathetic self,' Blitzwing sneers at Prime, 'when they wreak havoc in every human home, *you'll* get the blame!'

The Decepticon's fiery face suddenly spins back into his helmet – to be replaced with one of wild-eyed lunacy.

'Oooooo! Random mode! Aren't multiple personalities just *great!* A change is *so* refreshing, don't you think?'

As he advances, malice flashing in his mad eyes, the Pixie-6s follow in his wake.

To try to evade him, turn to 16.
To try to summon the other Autobots, turn to 24.

You soon find an entrance. It is spacious enough even for the Autobots – the entire facility has clearly been designed to allow the movement of large cargo. But it is sealed.

Bulkhead dangles a wrecking ball from one arm.

'Shall I knock?'

'Wait!' orders Prime. 'I'll override the locking system.'

He extends a finger, and a slim probe emerges from it. Prime stoops to insert it in a socket below the doorway's control panel.

Seconds later, the doors slide open. As they do so, Prowl makes a sudden lightning-fast movement, then holds up a clenched fist.

'What was that about?' asks Sari.

Prowl unclasps his hand. A tiny, spherical cam-bot lies on his palm.

'It was hovering just inside the passageway,' explains Prowl. 'Security 'bot. I took it off line before it could transmit.'

You're impressed with Prowl's ninja reflexes. You hadn't even seen it.

To examine the cam-bot more closely, turn to 89.

To follow the passageway, turn to 37.

It's impossible to get away – you are surrounded on all sides by Pixie-6 'bots, wielding their domestic tools as weapons.

'We need to destroy that control sphere!' growls Prime.

As Blitzwing prepares to attack, Prime suddenly snatches up both you and Sari, and fires the rocket-thrusters under his massive metal feet.

The giant Autobot shoots up towards the raised platform. But before he can reach it, Blitzwing stretches out and clutches his ankles. Prime extends his arms as far as he can, just enabling you and Sari to grab the edge of the platform before Blitzwing drags him back down to the ground.

With some effort, you haul yourself up on to the platform. The control sphere lies nearby.

Sari gives a frightened squeal. She is still clinging to the edge of the platform, unable to pull herself up.

To quickly grab the control sphere, turn to 63.
To hurry to help Sari, turn to 45.

Once the danger has passed, you and Sari emerge from your hiding place. Sari blows out her cheeks.

'That was too close for comfort! Let's get outta here!'

You quickly retrace your steps. Outside, your Autobot friends are waiting anxiously. Prime enthusiastically examines the evidence you've acquired.

'Good work. Molecular analysis of this should enable Ratchet to scan for matching compounds anywhere in Detroit. It might lead us to our culprit.'

'Where *is* Ratchet?' asks Sari.

'He's gone to the ship,' replies Prime, 'to see whether Teletran-1 picked up any telltale traces of activity in this area last night.'

Sari notices your blank look. 'Their spaceship is at the bottom of Lake Erie,' she explains. 'Teletran is its big supercomputer thingy.'

Prime turns to Bumblebee.

'If you vaporise the sample, Prowl can run a spectrograph of its composition with his high-definition olfactory sensors. We'll transmit the profile to Ratchet, and see if Teletran-1 can get a fix.'

'You mean – I zap it with my stingers, and Prowly sniffs it up?' simplifies Bumblebee. 'You got it!'

Within minutes, the sample's spectrogram has been transmitted. After a brief wait, Ratchet's gruff voice comes over Prime's comlink.

'That stuff's Cybertronian, for sure. And my scans are picking up only one match for it – has to be our bad guy. I'm asking Teletran to transmit a beacon signal to lead you there.'

'You heard the 'bot,' says Prime. 'Let's transform and roll out!'

Your four robotic companions rapidly assume their vehicle modes. Prime's fire truck rumbles up to you and Sari.

'You two did great – but I don't want to endanger you again. We'll take it from here.'

To accept Prime's decision, turn to 47.
To protest, turn to 28.

You pull up at the rear of the *HomeTech* laboratories. The street is deserted – apart from a large, green vehicle. As you approach, it changes into a truly colossal robot, with a powerful, barrel-shaped body.

Within seconds, your four mechanical companions are also back in robot mode, and are greeting the stranger warmly.

'Bulkhead!'

'Hi guys. Thought I'd find you here.' He turns to Prime. 'Your name's been all over the airwaves, boss. I've been eavesdropping on the police transmissions. According to them, you're meant to have broken into this place last night. They reckon they've got cam-bot footage to prove it.'

Prime looks puzzled.

'*HomeTech* release their latest home-helpbot next week,' continues Bulkhead. 'The Pixie-6. They've got advanced orders for millions of 'em – their aim is to place one in every home. The project is worth a fortune. The word is that you've been hired by another company to mess up the launch.'

Prime turns to you and Sari.

'We need to get hold of that security cam-bot footage, to see who really broke in last night. My friends and I are too big to investigate a facility of this kind undetected. Think you're up to it?'

There's a loud crash. Behind Prime, Bulkhead is casually swinging a heavy wrecking ball from one arm. A hole in the side of the *HomeTech* building now leads to a corridor within.

Bulkhead gives an innocent grin.

'Well lookie – there's even a back door…'

To follow the corridor to the left, turn to 38.

To go right, turn to 74.

As you reluctantly move away from Prime, one of Fanzone's officers takes aim with a bazooka-like weapon. But before he can fire, something slices through the air towards him. A triple-bladed *shuriken* – a ninja throwing knife – knocks the weapon from his grasp.

A moment later, a series of white energy bolts fizz past Prime's head and strike the hovering copter-bots. Several plummet to the ground, while the others buzz randomly about, out of control. The laser cage vanishes.

A yellow and black robot about half Prime's size rises from behind the police SWAT vehicle. With a whoop, he fires off another volley of energy bolts from his forearms, aiming well over the heads of the alarmed police.

Another robot – slightly taller, and black and gold – appears from nowhere, clutching two more *shuriken*.

'I'll keep them busy, Prowl!' yells the yellow robot. 'You and Optimus get out of here!' He rapidly changes into a fast-response cop car, and begins circling the bewildered police officers, engine revving wildly.

Something drops heavily from above you – one of the damaged copter-bots. Its blades catch your side.

As you stumble and fall, Prime stoops to scoop you

up. Straightening, he yells at the black and gold ninja-bot.

'You heard Bumblebee, Prowl! Move out!'

For the next few minutes you endure a rather rough ride in Prime's grasp as he beats a hasty retreat. The combination of the jogging motion and the throbbing pain in your side makes your journey a blur. You only regain focus when Prime eventually stops, and gently lays you down on a bench-like surface.

You try to take in your surroundings. A high ceiling; out of service production-line 'bots; a stack of rusting wheel hubs – it looks like some kind of disused factory.

To take a few moments to recover, turn to 34.
To try and sit up, turn to 92.

With Sari's paint-flake evidence safely stowed, you begin to make your way back towards the place where you entered the building. But you've barely left the coffee lounge when you spot a patrol of four security guard-bots.

Sari quickly pulls you through a side door before the 'bots see you – into a small storeroom packed with office supplies.

After a few minutes, you peer out cautiously. But the guard-bots are still there. They appear to be going over the whole area pretty thoroughly. You wonder if somebody somewhere is aware that there are intruders in the building.

'We'll never get back to Optimus and the others with them in our way,' grumbles Sari. 'We need to distract their attention somehow – to give ourselves a chance to get past. Either that or we just wait it out and keep our fingers crossed.'

To stay hidden and wait, turn to 9.

To try to think of a suitable diversion, turn to 25.

The moment you are clear of his cab, Prime changes back into robot mode. As a pair of missiles whoosh from beneath the wings of Blitzwing's fighter jet and rocket towards him, he pulls away the section of his chest armour that moments earlier formed his fire truck windscreen, and brandishes it like a shield.

Both missiles strike the shield, and explode. The double blast, though partly dispersed through the shield's ultra-tough armour, is enough to hurl Prime backwards into the wall behind him. The light in his eyes flickers then dies.

As Prime slumps to the floor, Blitzwing shape-shifts back into his hothead robot form. His expression is even fierier than before.

'Autobot down and out!' he screeches gleefully. 'I think that deserves a toast!'

He advances on you and Sari, his superheater cannon flaring.

'And you can be the toast!'

To try once more to evade him, turn to 41.
To plead with him, turn to 15.

As you approach the hole Bulkhead has just punched in the wall, Sari stops and turns to Prime.

'That news bulletin Bumblebee played back – it said one reason the police believed you might be trying to sabotage this 'Pixie-6' project was because they know you're friends with *me*, and *my* dad runs *HomeTech*'s main rival.'

'It did indeed, Sari,' replies Prime,

'Well, if they catch me sneaking around in their research laboratories, they're going to think it's even more likely that me, you and dad are mixed up in whatever's going on, aren't they?'

Prime nods.

Sari looks thoughtful for a moment, then shrugs.

'Guess we'll just have to make sure we don't get caught then, eh?'

Without further hesitation, she turns and leads you through the hole in the wall. You find yourself in a long, white-walled corridor.

To follow the corridor to the left, turn to 91.

To go right, turn to 82.

Your efforts are in vain. Blitzwing is closing in for the kill, when you hear a familiar robotic voice behind him.

'Oi – Weird-wings! Why don't you pick on someone your own size?'

Bulkhead has arrived on the scene. As Blitzwing spins to face him, the massive Autobot catches him on the jaw with a pile-driver fist.

The Decepticon staggers back, his three faces spinning in a blur.

Whirling a wrecking ball from his other arm, Bulkhead moves in for the knockout blow – only to be frozen solid by a sudden blast from the Decepticon's hyperfrost emitter.

'Very gallant, you big lump!' shrieks Blitzwing, now wearing the deranged expression of his Random mode. 'But now I think I'll have myself a little Autobot barbecue…'

He takes aim at the immobilised Bulkhead with his superheater cannon.

But before he can fire, a pair of *shuriken* – ninja throwing knives – come whistling through the air. The first blade strikes the control sphere up above. As the sphere shatters, the Pixie-6 'bots come to an immediate standstill.

The second *shuriken* hits Blitzwing behind the knees, sending him toppling backwards. As he falls, his scorching blast goes wildly astray, melting a large section of the metal ceiling. It collapses and falls – directly on top of the floundering Decepticon. The semi-molten metal sticks like fly paper. It quickly cools, re-solidifying, leaving an infuriated Blitzwing well and truly stuck.

As Prowl calmly retrieves his throwing knives, a yellow car screeches on to the scene and changes into Bumblebee. He aims a single stinger blast at Bulkhead. It shatters the big 'bot's ice jacket, enabling him to move again. Bumblebee strides towards you.

'You OK, kids? Sorry we didn't turn up sooner –'

He breaks off, having spotted Prime's prone form. Together, you hurry to where the Autobot leader lies, fearing the worst.

But Prime is OK.

'And thanks to you, my friends,' he says gratefully as he revives, 'I should no longer be a wanted 'bot. Now that we've exposed Blitzwing as the real *HomeTech* thief, we should all be in the clear.'

'Pity,' says Bumblebee, wistfully. 'I was getting to quite enjoy being an outlaw.'

His Autobot comrades cast him withering looks.

'What?' protests Bumblebee. 'Aww, come on – everybot likes a change now and then…'

THE END

As you try to evade Blitzwing, the Pixie-6 'bots begin to close in. Their makeshift weapons pose little threat to Prime – but they present a very real danger to you and Sari.

Prime hastily changes into fire truck mode, and flings open his cab doors.

'Get in!'

You and Sari gratefully take refuge in Prime's cab. He races away, ploughing through the ranks of Pixie-6s towards a clear area of floor. Reaching a dead end, he screeches round to confront the pursuing Decepticon.

'Do you call *that* an alt mode, Prime?' mocks Blitzwing. 'Pathetic! Let me show you a vehicle form *worth* taking…'

The Decepticon's body begins to fold, twist and shift. Moments later, he has assumed the shape of a sleek fighter jet, armed with an array of deadly missiles – already trained on Prime.

To warn Prime to move out of the jet's firing line, turn to 90.

To get out of his cab, fast, turn to 13.

Prime inclines his head once again.

'As you wish, my young friend. Go safely.'

But as he moves to leave, a yellow and black car comes racing in your direction. It swings off the skyway to come to a screeching halt beside you.

A small red-haired girl leaps from the car's passenger door. Ignoring you, she hurriedly addresses the towering robot.

'Optimus! You've gotta get outta here! I don't know what you're supposed to have done, but for some reason, the cops are after you!'

Prime gives her a puzzled look.

The girl turns back to the yellow car.

'Tell him, Bumblebee!'

For a second time, you witness an astonishing mechanical metamorphosis. The car suddenly becomes a shuffling mass of parts, rapidly taking the form of another giant robot – a little over half Prime's size. The newcomer speaks urgently to his fellow Autobot.

'Sari's right, boss. Captain Fanzone and half the Detroit Police Department are after your metal hide!'

The wail of approaching sirens confirms his words.

'Why should they want to arrest *me*?' frowns Prime. 'No matter – we had better move out. But we mustn't lead them back to base. Head for West 12 – where they're planning to build the new racebot arena. We can lie low there.'

'Gotcha!' replies Bumblebee. 'And I'll try to call up the other guys!'

Both massive robots rapidly change back into vehicle mode. Bumblebee pulls up beside you, opening a door for Sari – and you.

To get inside the car, turn to 88.
To stay put, to avoid getting involved in whatever trouble Prime is in, turn to 32.

Sari and Bumblebee haven't been gone long when Ratchet, checking on a flashing console alert, gives a worried grunt.

'We've got company. There's a patrol of police drones scanning right outside our front door.'

'They must have picked up Bumblebee's trail,' says Prowl. 'Will that 'bot *never* learn the value of stealth? If – '

'However they found their way here,' interrupts Ratchet, 'we can't let this young organic's life-signs lead them right to us – it'll blow our base's cover for good.'

You ask if there's another exit you could sneak out of.

'Possibly,' growls Ratchet. 'Or I could try making us invisible. A magnetic shield should hide us from the drones' sensors – long enough for us to get clear through the main entrance, anyway.'

His thick robotic wrists suddenly mutate. A glowing energy field begins to swell around each of them.

'Give an old 'bot a minute…'

To try Ratchet's plan, turn to 67.
To look for an alternative way out, turn to 2.

Unfortunately, Prime's impostor sees through your flattery. As Prime begins to struggle to his feet, his lookalike shimmers, revealing a purple and grey fighter jet instead. The jet swoops down from the platform, knocking Prime flat.

'It's Blitzwing!' says Sari, clearly horrified.

As the jet lands, it morphs into the form of a towering, stub-winged robot.

'Now I feel much more myself,' snarls the stranger. 'This holotech disguise is pretty effective, but I've been desperate to ditch all that revoltingly cheerful red and blue…'

'He's a Decepticon!' Sari hisses to you. 'Real nasty piece of work, with three attack modes – Ice, Fire and just plain bonkers.'

Judging by the chilling coldness in the Decepticon's eyes, you guess you're currently facing his icy persona. Your suspicions are confirmed as lethal-looking ice-spikes slide out from under the advancing robot's knuckles.

'And perhaps a little help from my troops…' he murmurs absently. He flashes his gaze up at the control sphere – still on the platform above. The Pixie-6s immediately begin to close in on you.

To retreat, fast, turn to 57.

To brace yourself for the Decepticon's attack, turn to 85.

You help Prowl and Bumblebee run memory scans on the remaining police 'bots – but without turning up any information about Prime.

Together, you head for the way out. A network of thin red beams crisscrosses the mouth of the exit tunnel.

'Motion detectors,' Prowl informs you. 'Best avoided.'

In a graceful sequence of gymnastic movements, he vaults, twists and cartwheels through the beams, somehow avoiding them all, despite his size.

'Yeah, yeah – very impressive,' scoffs Bumblebee. 'Now watch the master…'

He vaults the first sensor beam, lands clumsily, and tumbles through several others. Vertical plasma bars flare into life across the tunnel mouth, and an alarm begins to wail.

Prowl gives an exasperated sigh, then turns his attention to the now-blocked exit.

'I remember seeing the plasma generator on the outside wall,' he murmurs. 'I might be able to launch a *shuriken* through the bars to put it out of action.'

To try Prowl's plan, turn to 67.
To search for another exit, turn to 2.

You retrieve Prime's axe, but come under attack from the Pixie-6 'bots. As one lunges at Sari with a laser-peeler, she gives a squeal of fright.

'Optimus!'

But Prime has problems of his own. Without his axe, he is struggling to fend off his Decepticon look-alike.

With a mighty effort, he shoves Blitzwing backwards with his shield. Before the Decepticon can regain his balance, Prime deploys a set of climbing grips from one forearm, and uses this barbed arm to hook Blitzwing's legs from beneath him.

He hurries to your rescue, scattering the Pixie-6 'bots.

Blitzwing gets to his feet, looking more livid than ever.

'Enough of this pathetic Autobot get-up!'

He disables his holotech force-field and appears in his own robotic form.

'Let's see how you deal with the real me!'

To beat a hasty retreat, turn to 44.
To suggest to Prime that he change into
vehicle mode to get you out of here, turn to 68.

'Just a little something I put together to distract your simple-processored Autobot friends,' answers the giant robot. His red and blue robotic form may be identical to Prime's, but his voice, and the scornful look in his eyes, are all wrong. This isn't the Optimus Prime you know...

'He's the phoney!' Sari hisses at you. 'Now we're in trouble!'

She's right. As you back away, 'Prime' launches his rocket grapple, entangling you both in its line. He hauls you in, then takes hold of each of you in a crushing robotic grip.

'You might *look* like Optimus,' screams Sari, beating her fists angrily against her assailant's armoured hand, 'but he'd *never* be so cowardly as to pick on someone my size!'

'Silence, human!' roars the impostor. 'Cease your pathetic struggling, both of you – or do you want me to crush you here and now?'

To do as he demands, turn to 46.
To continue to put up a fight, turn to 4.

You soon discover what Sari means about her Key being unpredictable. As she applies it to the lock panel, it radiates a surge of light. But the door to the restricted area doesn't open. Instead, heavy doors suddenly seal each of the other corridors leading from the hub.

'See what I mean?' moans Sari. 'The problem with whatever the Allspark did to this thing is that along with its cool new powers, it's got a mind of its own!'

You're now left with no way out – except the central elevator. It looks like you'll have to try your luck on one of the upper floors.

'Shall I give it another go?' suggests Sari. 'Maybe it'll do the opposite this time, and switch all the doors to open – including this one.'

Or maybe, you think, it'll do whatever it feels like…

To continue your search on the next floor, turn to 91.
To try the Key again, turn to 71.

You open your mouth to yell for help, hoping to bring the other Autobots to your aid. But as you do so, Blitzwing fires a supercooling blast from his hyperfrost emitter. It misses you, but passes close enough to leave you numb with cold. Your jaw begins chattering so violently that you're unable to cry out.

Another hyperfrost blast catches Prime a glancing blow. He is lucky not to be totally immobilised. But the freezing effects of the Decepticon's weapon make his movement sluggish and awkward.

'Feeling a little chilly, are we?' taunts Blitzwing, with a sneer. 'Do allow me to warm you up a bit…'

As he advances, his hands become wreathed in flame.

'Talk about blowing hot and cold…' murmurs Sari. 'I think I like him least of all in Random mode!'

You back away awkwardly, your shivering limbs refusing to function properly.

To submit to the Decepticon, turn to 50.
To try to evade him as best you can, turn to 44.

Before you can come up with anything, help arrives – in the form of Prowl and Bumblebee.

The huge 'bots are far too large for the building's human-scale interior. But lack of space doesn't cramp their style. Several expertly thrown *shuriken* – ninja throwing knives – and a few warning stinger blasts soon encourage your assailants to retreat. Bumblebee sees them off, whooping like a cowboy, stingers blazing.

You quickly head for the nearest exit – only to see a security grille beginning to seal it.

In a flash, Prowl has changed into motorcycle form.

'Get on!' he urges.

You tear towards the lowering grille. As Prowl throws himself into a leaning side-skid, you and Sari flatten yourselves against his saddle – and just make it under.

'What about Bumblebee?' cries Sari, as Prowl pulls up. 'He's still inside!'

But a moment later there is a loud crash and Bumblebee, in car form, bursts from a first floor window. He changes in mid-air, hitting the ground in a neat forward roll.

'Not bad,' acknowledges Prowl, 'for one so

untrained in the art…'

You hurriedly produce the evidence you found in the lab. But Bumblebee cuts you off.

'Nice going – but we've already got the lead we need. That's why we came after you. Ratchet used Teletran-1 to tap into the traffic-cam system, on the off chance he could catch Prime's impostor in vehicle mode. He's got a positive fix, and he's transmitting a tracer signal.'

Bumblebee points to a red blip flashing on Prowl's dash.

'The others are already tailing it – we should catch them up.'

He rapidly changes into car form once more.

'Are you OK on old Prowl? Or would you rather travel in *real* style?'

To stay on Prowl with Sari, turn to 5.
To swap to ride in Bumblebee, turn to 77.

'How would you like to travel?' asks Prime. 'I can change back into vehicle mode if –'

He is interrupted by a sudden burst of sirens. Moments later, the sky around you is buzzing with police copter-bots – small flying robots that circle Prime's head like angry flies. Each 'bot in the swarm emits a single vertical laser beam. The ring of beams encircles Prime, trapping him where he is.

Several rapid-response police vehicles come speeding along the skyway and screech to a halt beside you. A police SWAT team spills from the largest vehicle. As its officers take up positions around Prime, a burly man with a large blond moustache squeezes out of the lead car. He looks up in satisfaction at the ensnared Autobot, and raises a megaphone to his mouth.

'This is Captain Fanzone of the Detroit Police Department. Optimus Prime, you are under arrest. I advise you to come quietly, or we will be obliged to use extreme force.'

Lowering his megaphone, the police captain speaks directly to you.

'Move away from the suspect, kid. We're gonna put him out for a bit with an EMP tranquilliser. You don't want to get in the way.'

To reluctantly do as Captain Fanzone says, turn to 11.
To stay close to Prime, in the hope it will prevent
the police using the tranquilliser, turn to 39.

Exploring the second floor, you find a door marked Security Control.

'Prowl was spot on,' says Sari. 'Betcha all the security cam-bots feed their data back to here. Dunno how we'll get in though…'

But to your surprise, the door isn't locked.

You quickly move to one of the control room's many touchscreens, and begin scanning for recordings from the previous night.

After several minutes fruitless searching, Sari gives a grunt of frustration.

'The cops must have downloaded the lot. Come on – let's get outta here.'

But from the inside, the door is locked.

'Clever!' says Sari. 'Why lock folk out when you can lock them in?'

She takes a device from around her neck.

'Maybe my Key will work…'

She presses the Key against a panel beside the door – and a hidden door in the opposite wall of the control room slides open.

To try the locked door again, turn to 71.
To follow the revealed corridor, turn to 74.

You have no intention of missing out on the action, and make this very clear to your Autobot friend. As Sari also protests, he backs down.

You're soon racing along the north-east highway out of the city. Through Bumblebee's windscreen, you can see Prime, Prowl and Bulkhead in convoy ahead of you.

Before long, your route leads you to the open water of Lake St. Clair. You're shocked to see the other Autobots veer from the road and head straight for the lake. Bumblebee, too, swerves to the left and races towards the water.

'Last one in is a Decepticon!'

All four vehicles plunge into the lake. As Bumblebee dives deeper, you're relieved to find that he seems watertight.

An amazing sight awaits you under the water. Sitting on the lakebed is a huge, hemispherical building.

'I've seen that on holo-vid!' says Sari. 'It's called the DeepDome. It belongs to *HomeTech*. It's where they keep all their finished 'bots. They built it underwater so their robo-sub freighters could run deliveries 24/7 without being affected by surface shipping.'

You can see a freighter moored at a nearby docking bay. Beside it is the entrance to a large airlock. Bumblebee follows the others through it.

The airlock's doors seal behind you and the water inside is rapidly expelled. As his fellow Autobots change into robot mode, Bumblebee carefully ejects you and Sari, and follows their lead.

The internal airlock door – designed to accommodate cargo containers – is large enough for even Bulkhead to fit through. It leads into a clear-walled tunnel running around the outside of the DeepDome's shell.

Bulkhead looks expectantly at Prime.

'Where now, Boss?'

To skirt the dome clockwise to find a way in, turn to 7.
To try the opposite direction, turn to 72.

You and Sari make a dash for it, leaving your robotic companion to deal with the police. Once out of the building, you sprint for the nearest skyway. Only after several minutes hard running do you halt, both out of puff.

There's no sign of pursuit.

'He'll… be… OK…' pants Sari. 'They're used… to this kind of thing. The Autobots. And they have a special place. To meet up. In emergencies.'

She sets off again, walking briskly.

Almost an hour later you find yourself approaching the barricaded entrance to a disused road tunnel.

'This is it.'

Sari leads you down into the tunnel. Parked in the semi-darkness are a fire truck, a medical response vehicle, a yellow police car, and a black and gold motorcycle. As you approach, all four vehicles change – into Optimus Prime, Ratchet, Bumblebee and Prowl, each crouching awkwardly under the tunnel's low ceiling.

'Thank the Allspark you're OK!' exclaims Prime. 'I still don't understand what the police want me for. But it seems they're happy to pull in my friends, too.'

'I think it's got something to do with *HomeTech*!' says Sari. 'You know – the big domestic robotics manufacturer. I've seen their boss guy in meetings with my Dad. And I spotted him back there, with the police!'

Prime nods his massive metal head.

'I know the *HomeTech* laboratories. Near the main solar plant. Perhaps we'll find an explanation there…'

Following his lead, his fellow Autobots change once more into vehicle mode.

To drive to the *HomeTech* lab in Ratchet, turn to 10.
To ride there on Prowl, turn to 35.

Despite his bravado, Bumblebee doesn't seem that 'OK' – the EMP blasts are coming thick and fast, and he is only just managing to deflect them all.

'This is when Prowl would tell me to 'find my inner calm' I guess!' he yells over the fizz and crackle of battle.

Sari notices your puzzled look.

'Prowl's another Autobot,' she explains. 'Black and gold, slim build, acts like some sort of ninja adept – you've probably seen him on the holo-vid news.'

One of Bumblebee's stingers goes wildly astray, blasting a hole in the building's wall. He's really beginning to struggle.

'Maybe we should wave the white flag,' he suggests, his stingers zapping madly as the onslaught continues. 'Before someone gets hurt.'

To surrender, as Bumblebee suggests, turn to 59.

To make a break for the hole in the wall, turn to 29.

Your desperate attempt to summon help pays off – the real Prime bursts on to the scene, axe drawn.

At the Autobot's appearance, his impostor releases you, and takes a step away. The lookalike shimmers before your eyes and it appears almost as if he is fading away. All traces of red and blue vanish, to be replaced by grey and purple. You realise it was a holographic field disguising a Decepticon. A helmeted robotic giant with stub wings and a fiery glare in his cruel eyes now confronts you.

'Blitzwing!' growls Prime. 'I should have known it was one of Megatron's Decepticon cronies who has been impersonating me. But to what end? And why break into the *HomeTech* laboratory?'

'For this!' snarls Blitzwing, holding up a small black sphere. 'But as to why – well, that's my little secret, isn't it?' He gives a deranged cackle.

'He's loopy!' Sari hisses to you. 'I've met him before. Or them, I should say. He's like three freaks rolled into one. Don't know which is most deadly – his Ice mode, the hothead one he's in now, or his Random mode, when he's just plain crazy!'

Blitzwing leers at you and Sari.

'I see you have some of your little pets with you,

Prime,' he sneers. 'I'm not keen on humans myself. Unless, of course…'

He suddenly launches a roaring fireball from one metal fist.

'… they're roasted!'

To dive out of the fireball's path, turn to 6.
To stick close to Prime, turn to 56.

'Come on – get in!' urges Sari. The sound of police sirens is getting ever louder. 'Bumblebee won't hurt you!'

A yellow robotic arm suddenly reaches from inside the car and gives you a firm shove in the back. You sprawl into the passenger seat. As the door slams shut, a seat belt wraps itself around you.

'Right! Hold on to your hydraulics!' says Bumblebee's voice, coming – bizarrely – from the dashboard.

As fire truck Prime roars away, Bumblebee sets off after him, tyres squealing.

You soon find yourself tearing across the part of town Prime had mentioned, where deserted buildings await demolition to make space for a giant new arena.

As you turn into an empty street, you find your route blocked by another massive robotic figure.

Prime and Bumblebee screech to a halt. As Prime swiftly changes, Bumblebee gently ejects you and Sari, and follows suit.

'Got your signal,' says the robotic stranger, gruffly. 'What's up?'

'Prime's in trouble with the law,' grins

Bumblebee.

'Why – what've you youngsters been up to now?'

Prime shrugs his massive metal shoulders.

The sound of sirens is growing louder again.

'Whatever it's about,' says Prime, 'I don't want these young humans caught up in it.' He turns to Bumblebee. 'Ratchet and I will try to lead the police away. Get these two out of sight.'

'I'm on it!'

Bumblebee quickly shepherds you towards the nearby entrance to a deserted multi-storey car park. Ramps lead to both the upper and lower levels.

'This looks like a good place to hide. What do you reckon, guys – up or down?'

To quickly climb the upper ramp, turn to 3.

To hurry down to the lower level, turn to 55.

You follow Sari cautiously into the *HomeTech* building.

Exploring the first few research areas reveals nothing about the break-in. In one, a white-coated 'bot-boffin is assembling a robot limb; in another, a team of young programmers are testing 'bot speech software. You sneak past, taking care not to be spotted.

You reach a place where several corridors join – a sort of hub, from the centre of which a magnetic elevator column rises to the upper floors. One corridor is sealed off. Its heavy door bears a bold security notice:

RESTRICTED ACCESS

PIXIE-6 PRODUCTION STAFF ONLY

The door itself looks rather the worse for wear – as though it has recently been forced.

'Now we're getting somewhere,' says Sari. But her face falls as she inspects the door's lock panel. 'Wish we'd brought that guard's pass-chip with us, though.'

She toys with the device around her neck.

'We could try my Key, I suppose – only it doesn't always do what you mean it to…'

To try Sari's Key, turn to 23.
To choose another corridor, turn to 74.

As you lie still, you hear the unfamiliar voice of a young girl.

'What have you been doing to the poor kid, you big metal lummoxes?'

A friendly, bright-eyed face appears directly above you.

'Hi! I'm Sari! You OK?'

Before you can answer, another voice interrupts. This time it's the synthetic speech of a robot, very low and gruff.

'Out of the way, little lady. I need to take a look at the patient.'

Sari's beaming face is replaced by the grizzled metal one of a tough-looking Autobot. He takes several minutes silently checking you over, then lays a heavy mechanical hand on your chest. It briefly emits a shimmering field of magnetic energy, and your pain subsides.

'You'll live,' grunts the Autobot.

You sit up – to find Prime, Bumblebee, Prowl and Sari all watching you anxiously.

'Nice work, Ratchet,' says Prime. 'You'd best keep an eye on our young friend here for a while. I need to find out why the police are so keen to take me in. Lie low until I report back.'

He changes back into fire truck mode, and heads for the plant's exit.

'Why does *he* get to do all the detective work?' grumbles Sari, as soon as Prime has gone. 'Hey, Bumblebee! You could run me over to the police HQ, couldn't you? Bet we could dig up something there to tell us why Optimus is a wanted 'bot!'

To go with Sari and Bumblebee, turn to 64.

To stay with Prowl and Ratchet, turn to 18.

Riding on Prowl is an exhilarating experience – if a little scary! You soon find yourself approaching a large white building. You pull into the shadow of its rear wall, where all four vehicles swiftly change into robot mode once more.

'Hey, boss,' says Bumblebee to Prime. 'Listen to this. Picked it up on the radio on the way here.'

Bumblebee's voice changes to that of a female newsreader.

'*Today's shock news – former city hero Optimus Prime is wanted by the police after breaking into the research laboratories of HomeTech, Detroit's second largest robotics manufacturer, last night.*'

'Not true!' protests Prime.

'*Prime is known to be friendly with the daughter of Isaac Sumdac, head of Sumdac Industries, HomeTech's main rival. HomeTech bosses accuse Prime of attempting to sabotage the eagerly anticipated launch of their latest product, the Pixie-6 home-helpbot.*'

'It must have been someone posing as me,' says Prime. 'But why?'

He turns to you and Sari.

'I'll need to identify the impostor, to clear my name. There may be evidence inside the labs. My friends and I are too large to snoop around – but you two could take a look.'

Bumblebee nudges him. A heavy green SWAT-type assault vehicle is rumbling your way.

'And here comes just the guy to help you make an entrance…' says Bumblebee.

As it draws near, the green vehicle becomes a blur of moving parts. A fifth, unfamiliar Autobot looms up before your eyes.

'Hey, Bulkhead!' Bumblebee gestures to the wall of the *HomeTech* building. 'How about a little remodelling, so our friends here can take a peek inside?'

The hulking green Autobot grins, aims a massive pile-driver fist at the wall, and effortlessly punches a door-sized opening in it.

To split up to search the lab, turn to 87.

To stick with Sari, turn to 14.

You and Sari accompany Prime, and soon find yourself in the largest area of the warehouse you have yet seen. Freight containers are stacked to its high ceiling all around.

There is a sudden whooshing sound. Prime stumbles and falls heavily, entangled in a net of clinging silver cable.

Suspended from the ceiling above is a maintenance platform. A giant robot that looks identical to Prime is leering down at you from it.

'You know, being you isn't *altogether* unbearable,' smirks the impostor. 'Some of your gadgets are really quite fun, aren't they? Of course, the *main* reason I adopted this holotech disguise as you,' he continues, 'was so *you'd* get the blame when I stole the control codes I needed to make this' – he holds up a small silver sphere – 'from the *HomeTech* labs. What does it do? I'll give you a little demonstration…'

He focuses his stare on the sphere. Suddenly, the cargo containers around you burst open. Thousands of small domestic robots begin to pour out. They fall into neat ranks, surrounding you.

'My own private army,' gloats the giant robot. 'With the stolen codes, this control sphere gives me remote command of each and every one of *HomeTech*'s delightful new machines. Imagine what that will mean when there's a Pixie-6 in every human home…'

You can see that Prime has managed to discretely shear through several of the net cables. If you can buy him some time by keeping his impostor talking, he might be able to free himself.

To ask the impostor who he *really* is, turn to 53.
To ask him to tell you more about his clever scheme, turn to 19.

The passageway leads to a fully-automated packing depot, in which a variety of worker 'bots are tirelessly and efficiently loading cargo containers. Each container is being filled with brand new, pre-packaged Pixie-6 'bots, arriving in a steady stream by maglev-conveyor.

There are several exits. As you pass one, Prowl pauses, and looks even more thoughtful than usual. You ask what's on his mind.

'My high-definition olfactory sensors are picking up an unusual odour. The faintest of traces – not more than one part in a trillion. But I'm almost certain it comes from an Energon-derived substance. Jet fuel, I think. And I detected an identical scent back in the *HomeTech* lab…'

'Could be our bad guy,' says Prime. 'Bulkhead, Bumblebee – go with Prowl and check it out.'

As the three Autobots hurry away, you notice that Sari isn't with you. She's probably snooping around the packing machines.

To ask Prime where she's gone, turn to 49.
To try to find her yourself, turn to 78.

As you make for the corridor, Sari stops, and turns back to Prime.

'This cam-bot recording – any idea where we might find it?'

Prowl steps forward.

'I may be able to help. The primitive devices used by humans to store digital video data give off a recognisable resonance frequency. My high-definition hearing should enable me to determine their location.'

He stoops to stick his head inside the building, listens intently for a few seconds, then withdraws it again.

'Unless my auditory sensors deceive me, the only video memory banks are in the facility's east wing, on the second or third floor.'

'Thanks, Prowl,' grins Sari. She turns back to the hole in the wall. 'So – heading left was right. If you see what I mean.'

You sneak inside, and quickly make your way to the east wing stairs.

'What do you reckon?' whispers Sari. 'Stick together, or take a floor each?'

To split up, turn to 87.

To stay with Sari, turn to 27.

You stand your ground beside Prime – but Captain Fanzone isn't about to let you mess up his planned arrest. He pulls a thick-barrelled firearm from inside his cop car, takes aim, and unleashes a pulse of crackling electromagnetic energy at the giant robot.

The energy pulse strikes you a glancing blow before Prime expertly deflects it with the head of his massive axe. With another swing of the axe's jet-powered blade, he takes out the entire host of copter-bots.

As you slump to the floor, you're vaguely aware of Prime stooping over you. There is a blur of mechanical activity around you, and you suddenly find yourself inside the cab of a fire truck.

'Time we moved out,' growls Prime's voice.

Your senses are still dulled by the energy pulse, but you are vaguely aware of Prime's bursts of acceleration and sudden changes of direction as you tear across the city. The truck only slows as it eventually rumbles through the entrance of a derelict industrial building.

Moments later, Prime has changed back into robot form, and holds you gently in a massive metal palm.

Inside the building – it looks like an old engineering plant – are two more giant robots. A sleek black and gold 'bot is meditating, cross-legged. His slightly smaller companion – yellow and black, and about half Prime's size – is absorbed in a zap-and-run holo-vid game.

'Bumblebee!' barks Prime. 'Fetch Ratchet – the child needs medical attention! Prowl – activate the medi-station!'

The smaller 'bot instantly changes into a speedy-looking car, and roars off down a nearby corridor. His companion – Prowl – moves swiftly to a control console, out of which slides a table-like slab.

Prime lays you gently down on the medi-station.

To take a moment to recover, as you're still dazed, turn to 34.

To get up immediately, turn to 92.

You and Sari do your best to assist Prime as he battles with his Decepticon enemy – but the two Cybertronians are on such a different scale, there's little you can do to tip the odds in your Autobot friend's favour.

Watching the two identical giant robots do battle is rather bizarre. The repeated crashes of mighty metal fist on tough Cyberium steel armour are deafening. As they grapple ferociously, the only way you can tell them apart is by the insane rage burning in Blitzwing's eyes.

Suddenly, the Decepticon gets the upper hand, as a scything stroke from his mighty ion-axe sends Prime's identical weapon clattering to the floor.

Disarmed, Prime quickly pulls away the section of his chest casing that doubles as a shield, and desperately tries to use it to deflect the fierce axe-blows that Blitzwing is now raining down on him.

To attempt to recover Prime's axe for him, turn to 21.
To yell at him to retreat, turn to 57.

You narrowly evade Blitzwing's next ferocious attack. But there's nowhere to run. Pixie-6 'bots, their domestic equipment deployed as weaponry, are advancing on all sides. And your Decepticon foe is already preparing another attack.

But hope is not lost.

In a flash of gold, Prowl drops to the floor nearby. He is clutching the control sphere, plucked from above. Strong-bot Bulkhead has arrived on the scene, too – he must have given Prowl the necessary boost to reach the sphere.

A yellow and black car comes clattering through the ranks of Pixie-6 'bots. It screeches to a halt, and morphs into the form of Bumblebee.

Prowl launches the control sphere in a high arc towards his fellow Autobot. A volley of energy bolts from Bumblebee's stingers catch the sphere in mid-air, blasting it to smithereens. Instantly, the entire host of Pixie-6 'bots comes to a standstill.

Blitzwing is enraged by the deactivation of his robot army. His triple visage spins wildly. With a howl of fury he unleashes icy blasts at all three of the newly arrived Autobots. Before they can defend themselves, Prowl, Bumblebee and Bulkhead are frozen to the spot.

The Decepticon turns his attention back to you and Sari.

'Your infernal friends have ruined my plans for global chaos!' he rants. 'Now you shall pay for their interference – with your lives!'

'I think not,' says a deep robotic voice.

Blitzwing spins, wide-eyed, to face Prime. Before the Decepticon can react, the recovered Autobot lands a mighty blow on his chin with the shaft of his ion-axe. Blitzwing is sent sprawling. And this time, he doesn't get up.

Prime quickly uses his grapple-line to bind his fallen enemy. Then he moves to his fellow Autobots, shattering the ice capsule in which each is entrapped with a careful axe-blow.

All four giant 'bots make their way towards you and Sari, looking battle-weary but happy. Sari grins up at Prime.

'When the police find out that Blitzwing was the real *HomeTech* thief, they should get off your case, Optimus!'

'Let's hope so, Sari,' smiles Prime.

'What about old Hot-n-Cold?' asks Bulkhead, gesturing to the unconscious Blitzwing. 'What happens to him?'

'We will attempt to amend his programming,' says Prime. 'He may yet renounce the malevolent influence of Megatron, and become a better 'bot.'

'A Decepticon?' says Bumblebee. 'Change into a good guy?' He gives a cynical chuckle. 'Now that's a transformation I'd really like to see…'

THE END

You slowly regain consciousness – to find three huge, anxious-looking metal faces looming over you.

Prime gives a sigh of relief.

'You're back online – thank the Allspark.'

Sari's face now also appears.

'Glad you're back. You were out for quite a while there!'

She helps you to your feet. You appear to be back outside, some distance from the *HomeTech* building. Sari sees your confused expression.

'Right after you blacked out, Prowl turned up. Says he sensed we were in trouble, so he came to get us out of there. He was awesome!'

'It was nothing,' says Prowl modestly.

A familiar yellow and black car comes roaring up, and morphs into the robotic form of Bumblebee.

'You OK, kid?'

You nod.

'Well, it was worth your trouble, guys. That evidence you found was top stuff! Ratchet and I went to run a few tests on it with Teletran-1 –'

'Their spaceship's computer,' Sari clarifies.

'– and it turns out it contains traces of a rare Energon isotope. Rare enough for Ratchet to scan for a local match.'

Bumblebee produces a hand-held display, on which you can see a blinking green dot.

'This tracker should lead us straight to our impostor.'

Prime is instantly spurred into action.

'Then what are we waiting for? Transform and roll out!'

To travel with Sari in Bumblebee, turn to 77.
To ride solo on Prowl, turn to 5.

You, Sari and Prime charge headlong at your Decepticon enemy. But before you reach him, the melting strands of the mesh net that binds his hands finally give way. As his hands come free, he gives a triumphant yell, and hurls his blazing missile straight at you.

The giant fireball roars your way, passing through the nearest ranks of Pixie-6s. The tiny 'bots are instantly fried, collapsing into small, sticky pools of molten metal and plastic. Sari screams as the ball of fire bears down on you.

But Prime is ready. His fire extinguishers burst into life, smothering the fireball with thick jets of fire-retardant foam.

Blitzwing curses angrily, draws his superheater cannon, and advances. As he stomps towards you, he skids awkwardly on the blanket of foam now coating the floor.

To get clear, while the slippery foam holds Blitzwing up, turn to 8.

To tell Prime to spray more foam at the Decepticon's feet, in the hope that he'll slip and fall, turn to 68.

Blitzwing laughs mockingly at your attempts to get away. Using the control sphere, he orders his Pixie-6 army to close in.

You follow in Prime's wake as he wades powerfully through the oncoming tide of 'bots. But when they close rank more swiftly behind him, you and Sari find yourselves cut off.

Sari, looking desperate, is nervously handling the Key around her neck. It suddenly glows with a powerful pulse of energy. A fierce white spark leaps from it to strike the nearest Pixie-6 'bot.

The spark jumps from one 'bot to the next, to the next. Each one emits a shower of smaller sparks, and becomes temporarily disorientated, coming to a standstill or spinning on the spot.

'It's stunning them!' says Sari.

But the first 'bot to be affected is already regaining control.

To tell her to try to activate the Key again, turn to 84.
To catch up with Prime before the other 'bots recover, turn to 62.

You haul Sari up over the platform's edge, where she takes a moment to catch her breath.

'Thanks… that was… interesting…'

There's a mad cackle from below. Blitzwing has changed into his 'Random' mode, and is gleefully bombarding Prime with alternate bolts of ice and flame.

Before you can grab the control sphere, Prime gives an urgent yell.

'Look out!'

From below, thirty or so Pixie-6 'bots are training their combined bug-zapper beam on the underside of the platform.

Prime fires his rocket-grapple into the ceiling above you. You and Sari grab its trailing line and swing from the platform. An instant later, the Pixie-6s find their mark, and its entire surface crackles with lethal electricity.

You slide down the grapple-line to the floor – to find Prime has paid a heavy price for saving your skins. He is out cold, floored by one of Blitzwing's wild blasts.

To try to bring Prime round, turn to 15.

To launch one last, desperate attack against Blitzwing, turn to 79.

You do as your giant captor commands, your mind searching frantically for a way out of your predicament.

It presents itself moments later – in the awesome form of the *real* Optimus Prime. Arriving on the scene, he processes the situation in a nanosecond, and charges headlong at your assailant.

The impostor releases you, in order to defend himself. But Prime hits his legs hard, bringing him down in a crunching tackle.

As the lookalikes grapple violently, the impostor shimmers, revealing a holographic field that has shaped itself around his robotic form. His red and blue casings resolve to purple and black as his body reveals itself to be a wiry, winged, evil-looking configuration.

'Blitzwing!' Sari hisses to you. 'He's a Decepticon. Real mean, and totally unstable. He's got three different attack modes. Ice, Random and – '

A sudden blaze of scorching flame erupts from the entire surface of the stranger's body, causing Prime to roll clear.

' – Fire!'

Prime gets to his feet beside you and Sari. His fiery adversary snatches up a small black sphere, bearing the *HomeTech* logo, which is rolling across the floor. Then he quickly rises to confront Prime.

'So that's what you broke into the lab for,' says Prime. 'What is it?'

'A primitive piece of human technology!' snarls the Decepticon. 'Rendered all-powerful by my own modifications! But it is no concern of yours or your puny human friends here…'

As he extends both forearms, a flame-thrower barrel erupts from each.

'…since you are about to fry!'

He launches twin streams of roaring flame straight at you.

To dive for cover, turn to 6.
To trust Prime to counter Blitzwing's attack,
turn to 56.

You may accept Prime's decision, but Sari certainly doesn't.

'We're all in this together! Besides…' – she clutches the electronic device around her neck – 'no me, no Key. And you never know when you might need *that!*'

She eventually gets her way. You are soon speeding along in Bumblebee after the convoy of other Autobot vehicles, hot on the trail of Prime's mystery impostor.

You come to a halt some distance out of the city. Bumblebee carefully ejects you and Sari and converts to robot form. His fellow Autobots have already changed.

Empty landscape stretches away on all sides. The air seems to have become suddenly cooler.

'But – there's nothing here…' you venture.

'Er… try looking *up*, youngster,' says Bulkhead kindly.

You do so, and catch your breath. A massive silver cube hovers a hundred metres above you, casting the huge shadow within which you are standing. A number of airborne vessels are moored to its underside.

'*HomeTech*'s storage facility,' says Prime. 'Where

they keep their finished 'bots ready for dispatch by rocket freighter. They call it the "wAirhouse".'

There's the sound of an engine. A medical response vehicle approaches, then rapidly converts into the grizzled form of Ratchet.

'That's where the traces lead, all right,' growls the veteran medi-bot. 'So I'd best get you lot up there.'

With a look of concentration, he extends his arms towards Prime. His thick wrists emit a shimmering field of magnetic energy, which surrounds the Autobot leader. Slowly, Ratchet raises the magnetic field, lifting Prime into the air.

Several minutes later, thanks to Ratchet's magnetic sky-lift, you find yourself standing alongside Sari, Prime, Prowl, Bulkhead and Bumblebee on the service gantry that runs around the wAirhouse's perimeter.

To seek an entrance along the gantry to the left, turn to 7.

To go right, turn to 72.

You and Sari rush forward with Prime, hoping to help finish off his Decepticon opponent.

But suddenly the floor beneath you turns to sheet ice. Your arms and legs flail wildly, and all three of you crash to the ground. Prime's shield clatters from his grasp as he falls, coming to rest on the ice just beside you and Sari.

You struggle to get up, but it's impossible to keep your feet on the slippery surface.

Blitzwing has now recovered. He laughs cruelly as he watches your attempts to stay upright. A cylindrical device protrudes from his right forearm, giving off a hazy smoke like dry ice.

'How do you like the work of my hyperfrost emitter?' he gloats. 'Cool, isn't it?'

He aims the device directly at you.

To try to take cover behind Prime's dropped shield, turn to 68.

To scramble away as best you can, off the ice sheet, turn to 57.

Prime is more than a little concerned at Sari's disappearance.

'Wait here while I find her,' he says firmly. 'And don't move.'

He hurriedly crosses the packing area, scanning for Sari. You watch him duck into the first of the area's several side annexes.

Only seconds later, Sari comes cheerfully scurrying up.

'This place is fab! Where are Optimus and the others?'

Before you can answer, a huge metal hand seizes you from behind. Its grip closes tightly around you, one finger sealing your mouth before you can yell.

A second giant hand has Sari in its grasp, muffling her angry protests.

The hands lift and rotate, and you find yourselves staring into a huge robotic face. Prime's face – but with an unfamiliar cruelty in its eyes.

To try to struggle free, turn to 4.

To kick out at your captor's metal casing, in the hope that the noise might draw the real Prime's attention, turn to 31.

You may be ready to surrender, but Prime isn't. As the heat given off by his approaching enemy helps to thaw his frost-jammed mechanisms, the Autobot takes action. He deploys his fire extinguisher, and sprays a thick jet of fire-retardant foam at Blitzwing's blazing hands.

The Decepticon lifts his now-smouldering fists with a livid snarl.

'You Autobots just don't know when to quit, do you?'

'On the contrary,' replies Prime. 'I know exactly when to quit. Never.'

Blitzwing's response is a series of ferocious blasts from his superheater cannon. As his fiery missiles roar your way, Prime picks off each one with a well-aimed shot of extinguisher foam.

A good deal of Prime's foam spray hits the Decepticon. It clearly infuriates him – he breaks off his attack to swipe some of it angrily away.

To run for it, while Blitzwing is distracted, turn to 16.
To tell Prime to foam his face, so he can't see,
turn to 68.

'I imagine your idiotic Autobot friends are scurrying about after their foolish leader,' snarls the giant red and blue robot, in answer to your question. He may look like Prime, but his voice – and manner – is all wrong.

'That was certainly the aim of my diversion,' continues the impostor menacingly. 'To draw them away so that we could get better acquainted.'

He stoops to bring his massive face close to Sari's.

'You see, I have a certain interest in that Key of yours…'

Sari clutches the device around her neck protectively, and yells at you.

'Run!'

But before either of you can move, Prime's impostor has drawn his massive axe. Holding its long shaft at either end, he uses it to pin both you and Sari against the wall.

'Oh, I don't think you're going anywhere in a hurry,' sneers your assailant. 'Do you?'

To try to squirm free, turn to 4.
To shout for help, turn to 31.

You can't get Prime's attention – he's busy listening to the guard.

'It was you! I saw you with my own eyes! You broke into the labs last night, and when we tried to take you in, you knocked poor Charlie out cold!'

Prime frowns, mystified. The guard continues.

'It's all about the Pixie-6s isn't it? When they launch next month, it'll be *HomeTech*'s biggest deal ever! We've been making millions of 'em – the world's ultimate home-helpbot! They'll be in every home before the year is out! Except someone's hired you to sabotage the project, haven't they?'

Shaking his head in puzzlement, Prime turns to Ratchet.

'Give this human something to calm him, Ratchet.'

Ratchet grunts.

'Dunno what works on organics. Maybe a shot of Energon-suppressant?'

A long-needled syringe slides out from under one of his mechanical knuckles. At the sight of it, the guard slumps down in a dead faint.

'That seems to have done the trick,' says Prime. 'Keep an eye on him.'

Ratchet nods, and immediately changes into his

alternate mode – a medical response vehicle. Bulkhead gently lifts the unconscious guard inside Ratchet's rear doors, and the medi-bot pulls away.

'I'll take a look around outside,' says Bulkhead. He too changes – into a SWAT assault vehicle – and rumbles away.

Prime un-shoulders his massive axe, and moves to the wall of the *HomeTech* building.

'If I'm to clear my name, we need to find out who really broke in here last night.'

He uses the axe blade to prise away a ventilation grille near the wall's base. Through the revealed opening – just about large enough for you to crawl through – you can see a corridor within.

Prime turns to you and Sari.

'How about a spot of detective work?'

To crawl inside the *HomeTech* building, turn to 91.
To let Sari go first, turn to 33.

In answer to your question, Prime's impostor undergoes a radical transformation. A holographic field that had shaped itself around the robot's form shimmers and fades away. Red and blue gives way to purple and grey. You find yourself looking up at a giant stub-winged robot with a chillingly frosty demeanour.

'I am Blitzwing!' declares the stranger. 'Loyal follower of Megatron, true leader of the Decepticons!'

'We've met before,' Sari hisses to you. 'Total fruitcake.'

Blitzwing stoops to put down the control sphere, then traces a curve through the air with one outstretched arm. Wherever he points, the moisture in the air instantly freezes, creating a spiralling slide of solid ice. The Decepticon swiftly uses it to descend from the platform.

But by now, Prime is on his feet. As Blitzwing reaches the floor, Prime catches him with a blow from his axe shaft. Blitzwing staggers backwards, howling with rage. His visage suddenly changes from icy cold to fiery hot. A wave of heat surges from him, instantly vaporising the ice slide.

'He's kinda got a split personality!' explains Sari.

'Has Cold, Hot and Random modes. Prime's got him all fired up!'

As she speaks, the Decepticon begins to conjure a giant fireball with his metal hands. You see his gaze flash up at the control sphere above. The Pixie-6 'bots come alive, and begin to advance.

To keep out of the Pixie-6s reach, turn to 8.

To focus on Blitzwing, turn to 73.

As you seek cover behind him, Prime quickly seizes his mighty ion-axe – not a moment too soon. The left barrel of Blitzwing's tank turret recoils as it unleashes a high-velocity shell straight at you.

With lightning reactions, Prime slices his axe blade across, deflecting the deadly missile. It ricochets away to explode against the wall behind you.

But Blitzwing's second gun fires before Prime has time to recover. It strikes the towering Autobot full in the chest. The explosive impact sends him sprawling across the floor.

Blitzwing's tank dissolves into a blur of moving mechanical parts as he changes back to his fiery robot form. He cackles malevolently as he advances once more.

'Now I'm really having a blast!'

Prime's ion-axe lies beside his prone body. You wonder whether you and Sari could lift it between you.

To try to use the axe to attack Blitzwing, turn to 79.
To scramble clear, turn to 41.

The lower level turns out to be a bad choice. No sooner have you reached it than you are confronted by a police patrol of a dozen officers, armed with EMP tranquilliser guns. They are led by a broad-chested, impressively-moustached officer who seems a little out of breath.

'Captain Fanzone!' Bumblebee greets him innocently, shielding you and Sari behind his robotic body. 'What brings you here?'

'Where's Prime?' scowls Fanzone. 'I have a warrant for his arrest.'

'Optimus?' Bumblebee looks thoughtful. 'Oooo, now let me see… When was the last time I saw Optimus…?'

Captain Fanzone clearly has no time for messing about.

'Knock him out,' he barks at his armed colleagues. 'We'll take him in for questioning, too.'

As a barrage of tranquilliser pulses comes fizzing your way, Bumblebee's robotic arms instantly convert. With lightning speed, he unleashes a volley of return blasts from their glowing tips – not aiming at the officers, but expertly picking off each of the approaching energy bolts.

'I said shoot him!' yells Fanzone, red-faced.

But as the energy bolts come thicker and faster, Bumblebee's sharp-shooting continues to prevent any of them scoring a hit.

There's a door marked EMERGENCY EXIT in the wall to your left.

'You two get out of here!' urges Bumblebee, picking off yet another oncoming shot. 'I'll be OK!'

To make a dash for the exit, turn to 75.

To stick it out with Bumblebee, turn to 30.

As Blitzwing's fiery attack roars towards you, Prime activates his arm-mounted extinguishers and stifles the blast.

'Very impressive!' snarls the Decepticon. 'I'd love to stick around, but you know how it is – must fly!'

His mechanical body changes once more – into the shape of a heavily armed fighter jet.

'Down!' yells Prime, pressing you to the floor.

A pair of missiles rocket from under the jet's wings, tear narrowly past you, and blow a massive hole in the opposite wall. With a roar of engines, the fighter plane zooms after them.

You scramble to your feet and quickly give chase. The hole in the wall leads into a cavernous warehouse chamber. Blitzwing – now in his icy robotic mode – is standing at its centre. He is flanked by row upon row of Pixie-6 helpbots.

In the Decepticon's outstretched palm lies the mysterious sphere. He somehow creates a coating of ice around it, then tosses it up to cling to the chamber's high ceiling.

'With my modifications, the control sphere enables me to remotely command all these charming little 'bots,' gloats Blitzwing.

He directs a frosty stare at the sphere suspended

up above. As he does so, each Pixie-6 'bot suddenly deploys one of its domestic tools. From cutting-wheels to bug-zappers, all are brandished by the little 'bots in weapon-like fashion. You have the impression of an army preparing for battle.

'Imagine what that will mean when there's a Pixie-6 in every home,' continues the Decepticon gleefully. 'And thanks to my newly acquired holotech disguise…'

He engages the holographic field again, becoming Prime's double once more.

'…everyone will blame *you* for the chaos I create!'

With a demonic cackle, he begins to advance, backed by his Pixie-6 army.

To help Prime take on his evil double, turn to 40.
To get well out of the way, turn to 44.

Try as you might to get away, Blitzwing pursues you menacingly.

'Oh, what the heck!' yells Sari, turning to face him. 'Attack's the best form of defence. *Geronimo!!!*'

She rushes at the massive Decepticon, and wraps herself around one of his powerful legs. Heart pounding, you charge at the other.

You have no chance of toppling the giant robot, but your unexpected attack distracts him momentarily – long enough for Prime to plant a powerful punch on his jaw. As Blitzwing stumbles backwards, crushing several of his Pixie-6 infantry, you and Sari scramble clear.

The Decepticon's multiple faces spin wildly, from fiery, to icy cold, to mad-eyed.

'Right!' he screeches insanely. 'If that's how you want it – time to bring on the big guns!'

He swiftly changes, this time into an awesome attack tank. The twin barrels of its gun turret quickly zero in on their target – you.

To hit the deck, turn to 60.
To take cover behind Prime, turn to 54.

Sari giggles as you mimic Prowl's meditative pose. But her smile fades at the sound of eager electronic yapping – the dog-bot patrol is coming back.

The police officers' approach brings Prowl instantly out of his trance. He springs to his feet and draws a pair of triple-bladed throwing knives – ninja *shuriken* – from behind his back.

The approaching dog-bots switch to attack mode. As they bound towards you, their mechanical jaws crackle with electric energy – one bite will put you out for the count.

But Prowl has other ideas. He launches his gleaming *shuriken* with deadly accuracy, silencing both canine 'bots.

The officers have called for backup – you can see reinforcements approaching. Prowl calmly adopts a defensive ninja stance, but looks uneasy.

'I cannot engage them fully without the risk of harming them.' He gestures to a nearby fire escape. 'But I may be able to buy you a little time…'

To dash for the fire escape, turn to 29.
To turn yourselves in, turn to 59.

You are about to turn yourselves in, when suddenly the wall beside you explodes. A large vehicle crashes through it, sending a hail of rubble towards the startled police. As they take cover, the red and blue truck screeches to a halt, then rapidly changes. Moments later, Optimus Prime is towering over you.

Prime stoops to grab you and Sari, then speaks urgently to your robotic companion.

'Head for the emergency rendezvous!'

As Prime turns and strides through the gaping hole he has created, the police open fire. But Prime's pace is awesome. You watch buildings pass in a blur as he thunders away from danger, closely followed by his fellow Autobot.

Your escape route eventually leads to a large, derelict furniture warehouse. Inside, the other Autobots are waiting anxiously. Prime puts you and Sari down gently, then turns to address them.

'You got my signal. Good. Has anybot discovered yet why the police are so keen to talk to me?'

'I picked up a few sound-bites from the ether,' drawls Prowl. 'Your name repeatedly mentioned in connection with something called "*HomeTech*"...'

Sari's face lights up.

'That's the big robotics company near the Speedball Stadium! Dad says their stuff's pretty cool!'

'Then that's our next destination,' replies Prime. 'Transform and roll out!'

All four robots swiftly convert into vehicle mode – Ratchet becoming a medical response vehicle, Prowl a sleek police motorcycle, and Prime and Bumblebee the familiar fire truck and unmarked cop car.

Both Bumblebee and Prowl pull alongside you, engines purring.

To hitch a lift inside Bumblebee, turn to 10.
To climb astride Prowl, turn to 35.

As you dive for the floor, fully expecting to be blasted by Blitzwing's tank guns at any moment, Prime acts with impressive speed. In a blur of mechanical shape-shifting, he morphs into his fire truck alt mode, and hurtles straight at his Decepticon enemy.

There's an almighty crash as the two heavy vehicles collide head-on, scattering Pixie-6 'bots around them. The force of the impact sends a tremor across the whole area. As silence falls, you scramble to your feet, and hurry to see if Prime is OK.

Both giant 'bots are in the process of reverting, with some difficulty, to robot form. Blitzwing is the first to complete his transformation. He staggers to one side, shaking his helmeted head, clearly dazed.

But he's in better shape than Prime. The Autobot just about manages to resume his robot form, before collapsing to the floor.

To try to revive Prime, turn to 15.

To attack Blitzwing while he is still dazed, turn to 79.

Bulkhead has no trouble forcing open one of the cargo containers. Inside, you find thirty or so transparent pods, each holding a shiny new home-helpbot.

Bulkhead removes one of the pods, cracks it open, and lifts out the little robot inside.

'Funny to think that until us Autobots dropped in,' he says to Sari, 'you humans thought that 'bots like these performing monkeys were the pinnacle of robot engineering…'

Sari looks defensive.

'Hey, I know they're not sentient, like you guys,' she admits, 'but they're still pretty neat.'

She prises open a panel in the back of the Pixie-6, and starts examining the complex electronics within.

'Dad would be very interested in a sneak preview of what makes these latest generation *HomeTech* 'bots tick…'

'Er, guys…'

Bumblebee is waiting with Prime and Prowl, clearly impatient to set off along the passageway.

'Shouldn't we be, you know, catching villains?'

To hurry Sari along, turn to 72.

To wait while she finishes her examination, turn to 65.

As you move to join Prime, a powerful jet of thick white foam sends you and Sari sprawling helplessly across the floor. You hear Blitzwing's demonic cackle, and squirm around to confront an exact duplicate of Prime's fire truck mode.

'You see,' says the Decepticon's snide voice, 'this holotech has been developed to adopt any form I choose. Luckily, I included your dear Autobot friend's vehicle mode in my programming.'

You attempt to get back on your feet, but the fire truck's extinguisher emits another jet of fire-retardant, sending you skidding across the floor once more.

'Oh, this is fun!' mocks Blitzwing.

You're relieved to see Prime hurrying back to help you – until his huge feet skid on the foamy floor, and he falls heavily. He doesn't get up.

Blitzwing resumes his robot form. He advances, his faces spinning dementedly.

To throw all your strength into one last desperate attack, turn to 79.
To scramble away, turn to 41.

As you snatch the control sphere, Blitzwing gives a screech of anger, and his eyes fill with fire. The sphere suddenly becomes unbearably hot. With an agonised yell, you drop it again.

The Decepticon hurls Prime aside, then unleashes a roaring blast from his superheater cannon – straight up at the platform.

The stream of fire hits the underside of the platform, instantly making its surface red-hot. You have no choice but to leap into thin air. Sari gives a piercing scream as she, too, falls.

Yet again, Prime is your saviour. In a split second, he launches a capsule from his shoulder. It bursts apart, inflating into a huge airbag, which breaks your fall.

In saving you and Sari, Prime has left himself open to attack. Blitzwing catches him with a flaming fist. The Autobot goes down heavily – and doesn't get up.

With Prime out of action, Blitzwing turns his attention back to you and Sari.

To try to revive Prime, turn to 15.
To run for it, turn to 41.

At the Detroit Police Department headquarters, a couple of well-aimed blasts from Bumblebee's laser-like stingers take out two of the security cambots, enabling you to get close to the building. Two more silent stinger shots deactivate the electronic locks of a ground floor office window.

You soon find yourself inside the police building – in a largish, unoccupied office – hastily scanning through criminal data files with Sari. You're looking for anything that might explain why Prime is wanted by the cops. Bumblebee anxiously keeps watch outside the open window.

'Oops!' exclaims Sari. The touchscreen she's been using suddenly begins flashing dramatically. 'Think I just tried to get into some restricted-access stuff…'

Seconds later, the door bursts open, and four armed officers charge in. You back against the wall as they level their plasma weapons at you threateningly.

To give yourselves up, turn to 59.

To make a break for the window, turn to 29.

Sari is keen to give the Pixie-6 a good look over. After a childhood surrounded by robot technology – in her father's workshops, home and factory – she certainly knows her way around a circuit board. As she busily dismantles the *HomeTech* 'bot, Prime speaks to his fellow Autobots.

'You three go on ahead. I'll keep an eye on these two. We'll rejoin you as soon as Sari's through tinkering.'

As Prowl, Bulkhead and Bumblebee hurry away, you watch Sari – now thoroughly absorbed in her work – explore the Pixie-6s robotic anatomy. Prime, meanwhile, takes the opportunity to have a better look around.

Minutes later, he rejoins you and Sari.

'There's another passageway over there. Its entrance is concealed. My sensors are picking up faint traces of Energon activity from that direction. I intended to rejoin the others – but I wonder whether we should investigate first…'

To catch up with the other Autobots, turn to 37.
To explore the concealed passageway, turn to 36.

The room you enter has two levels. A flight of metal steps leads to a mezzanine floor. Several of them are badly bent — someone extremely heavy has recently climbed them. You follow in their destructive footsteps.

At the far end of the mezzanine stands a heavy black cabinet — a safe. Its door, like those of the room itself, has been badly damaged, forced open despite numerous hi tech, heavy-duty locking mechanisms.

A glint of something metallic on the floor beside the raided safe catches your eye. You stoop to pick up a small fragment of 'bot-armour. Evidence.

Suddenly, Sari bursts on to the scene.

'Quick! Hide!' she squeals. 'I got spotted! There's a squad of guard-bots right behind me!'

You can hear them rattling up the steps. You look over the mezzanine's side, wondering if you and Sari could drop to the floor below to make a getaway. It's a risky jump — you could easily knock yourself out.

To hide inside the safe, turn to 9.
To brave the jump, turn to 42.

To your relief, the plan works, and you are able to escape the building. But you have only seconds to enjoy your relief before a frown creases Prowl's metallic brows.

'I'm picking up an alert from Bulkhead. Time to move out.'

Before you can ask who Bulkhead is, your robotic companions have both changed into vehicle mode. Prowl – now a sleek black and gold motorcycle – pulls up alongside you, clearly intending you to get on.

What follows is the ride of your life – a blur of speed and rushing air. Several hair-raising minutes later, you find yourself dismounting, legs trembling, in the shadow of a massive white hexagonal building. A logo on its otherwise featureless side reads *HomeTech*.

Both your robotic companions change back into robot mode. Their fellow Autobots, and Sari, are already gathered outside the building.

As you join them, you notice two strangers in the group – a terrified-looking man in a security officer's uniform and, towering over him, a colossal green Autobot you've not seen before. You guess the robot must be Bulkhead.

To ask Sari what's going on, turn to 83.
To talk to Prime, turn to 52.

Before you can put your plan into action, the other Autobots suddenly burst on to the scene. Bumblebee and Bulkhead hurry to their leader's side. Prowl swiftly changes into his motorcycle alt mode, and comes tearing your way, slicing through the ranks of Pixie-6 'bots.

'Jump on!'

With you and Sari clinging to his saddle, he zooms towards the relative safety of an area clear of Pixie-6s.

Meanwhile, even the combined offensive efforts of Prime, Bumblebee and Bulkhead are having little effect on Blitzwing, The deranged Decepticon, who is now changing his robot mode every few seconds, is subjecting the struggling Autobots to a ferocious barrage of ice and fire attacks.

Sidestepping a blast from the Decepticon's hyperfrost emitter, Prime launches his grapple-line at the control sphere up above. He hurriedly reels in the line, and catches the sphere as it falls.

'Think you can control my army, do you?' sneers Blitzwing, forcing all three Autobots back with the raking fire of his superheater cannon. 'Don't waste your time! That control interface links only to my neural circuits!'

He levels his weapon at Prime.

'Now – GIVE IT TO ME!'

'Whoa! Chill a little, Mister Hotbot!' taunts Bumblebee.

He takes the sphere from Prime.

'You say this thing's linked to your neural circuits? Then I'd guess this is really gonna sting…'

He quickly fires a stinger bolt directly into the control sphere's data-port. As the sphere blazes with energy, the same fierce white light flares behind Blitzwing's mad eyes. He collapses, out cold. The Pixie-6 'bots come to a standstill.

Bulkhead lets out a sigh of relief, and lays a massive metal hand on Bumblebee's shoulder.

'Nice going, little guy.'

He takes the control sphere – no longer aglow – from his fellow Autobot. Closing his powerful fist around it, he crushes it into fine black powder.

'A most satisfying resolution,' says Prime. 'Once we've informed the police of Blitzwing's scheme, my name should be cleared.' He turns to you. 'Which means I can take you home – as I promised some time ago.'

He surveys the aftermath of your recent battle.

'But first, we must restore order to this facility.'

'Maybe we could recruit a little help…?' suggests Bulkhead, looking meaningfully at the thousands of Pixie-6 'bots.

Prime gives a wry smile.

'I think they've 'helped' enough for one day – don't you…?'

THE END

As you head for the exit, an alarm wails into life. Armed police come swarming on to the scene.

The lead officer reports into his comlink.

'Intruders apprehended in Sector 4. One Autobot, known associate of fugitive Optimus Prime. Two human juveniles. Request net-bot unit to restrain the robot. Will use stun guns to neutralise the youngsters.'

On his signal, his fellow officers take aim at you and Sari.

In an instant, Ratchet has raised both massive hands to project a wall of magnetic energy in front of you. As the first burst of stun gun fire hits it, the pulses ricochet away.

'I could wade right through this little lot,' grumbles the veteran Autobot, as you are driven back against a wall. 'But not without exposing you.'

A deflected pulse sends a police officer sprawling.

'I guess we'd better turn ourselves in before anyone gets hurt – unless you two think you can make it to the exit…'

To give yourself up, turn to 59.

To make a dash for the exit, turn to 29.

As you bide your time, Sari suddenly appears through the damaged doorway. You *psssst!* to her, and she rushes to join you.

'I thought I was gonna be stuck in there forever! There are cops all over the place. But look, I found some evidence at last…'

She holds out her palm to show you a smear of green gel.

'It's the same type of lubricant I've seen Prowl treat his joints with,' says Sari. 'Whoever broke in left behind a smudge of it when he trashed the room through there. The police hadn't spotted it. Don't think they spotted me when I grabbed it, either.'

'Wrong, missy,' says a deep voice behind you. You spin to face two officers with their laser handguns trained on you.

'They're just kids, Zac,' says one to the other. 'Make sure you're set to stun.'

To quickly come up with an excuse for your presence, turn to 25.

To run for it, and chance the stun guns, turn to 42.

Thankfully, Sari's Key works, and you are able to continue exploring the *HomeTech* building. But minutes later, as you try to enter another restricted area, you trigger the security systems.

As the alarms blare, you and Sari sprint for the place where you gained entry. You make it outside – to find only Bumblebee still there. He is waiting anxiously in vehicle mode, doors open and engine revving.

As you and Sari slip gratefully into his seats, dog-bots burst from the building behind you. Before they can reach you, Bumblebee roars away at top speed.

'I'm sorry, Bumblebee,' says Sari, downhearted despite your narrow escape. 'We didn't find any clue as to who broke in back there.'

'No worries,' says Bumblebee cheerfully. 'After you went in, old Mister Supersenses – Prowl – sniffed out an Energon signature trace around the front of the site.'

You and Sari look blank.

'It's kinda like an electromagnetic scent,' explains Bumblebee. 'Ratchet's gone back to HQ to try to find a match for it. The others have just rolled out to see where the trail leads. Optimus told me to wait for you two, then see you home safely. He reckons he's already put you in enough danger.'

To accept Prime's decision, turn to 47.
To kick up a fuss about missing the action, turn to 28.

It isn't long before you've found your way into the heart of *HomeTech*'s state-of-the-art warehouse. As you move through an area occupied by robotic packing machinery, currently inactive, Bumblebee accidentally catches a stack of packaging pods, sending them tumbling noisily to the floor.

Prowl gives him a withering look.

'Will you ever grasp the concept of stealth, I wonder?' he drawls.

Bumblebee looks rather crestfallen as you continue your search.

Suddenly, there's a further series of loud crashes.

'It wasn't me!' protests Bumblebee.

'No – it came from another area,' agrees Prime. 'Somewhere up ahead. Perhaps it's my impostor!'

He turns and speaks firmly to you and Sari.

'Stay here while we check it out!'

As all four Autobots sprint away, Sari has a good grumble – something about being treated like a baby. But almost immediately, Prime returns, looking rather bad-tempered.

To ask him where the others are, turn to 51.

To ask what the noise was all about, turn to 22.

As Blitzwing's deadly fireball swells in size, Prime takes action. He raises his mighty right arm. The mechanical components that form its foremost part split open as his net-gun device springs from its casing.

Prime quickly takes aim, and the net-gun spits out a small web of tough Cyberium steel mesh, which flies towards the Decepticon. The mesh net wraps itself around Blitzwing's hands, preventing him from releasing his fiery missile.

'Nice shot, Optimus!' squeals Sari.

The infuriated Decepticon lets out a roar of rage.

'Your puny Autobot gadgets cannot contain the wrath of a Decepticon!'

His eyes blaze as he concentrates his fiery powers. The fireball grows greater still, becoming so ultra-hot that the mesh of the net gradually begins to melt.

To attack the Decepticon while his hands are still bound, turn to 43.

To run for it before he can retaliate, turn to 16.

You haven't gone far along the corridor when you come to a place where a large section of the outside wall has been smashed inwards, leaving a gaping hole.

'Looks like this is where our intruder got in,' says Sari. 'They were about Prime's size, too, judging by the scale of the damage!'

Silver columns stand on either side of the ragged opening. Spanning the gap between them is a grille of horizontal beams of blue light. The luminous grille covers the breach in the wall completely.

'Someone's set that up as a temporary barrier, I guess,' says Sari. 'Till the wall's fixed. They're probably stun beams – to stop any more unwelcome visitors sneaking in uninvited.'

You wonder if there's any clue here as to who last night's mystery intruder might have been, and what they were after.

To search the debris for clues, turn to 86.

To take a closer look at the entry hole itself, turn to 80.

Only Sari makes it to the exit – you find yourself pinned down by more EMP fire. She looks back, clearly reluctant to make her escape without you.

'I'll fetch help!' she yells, then ducks through the exit.

But help comes even sooner than Sari could have hoped. Moments after she leaves, a giant figure cartwheels on to the scene, moving so fast that he is little more than a black and gold blur. With a series of lightning kicks, he knocks the tranquilliser weapons from the grasp of each attacking officer, then back-flips, ninja-like, to join you and Bumblebee.

Captain Fanzone looks less certain about taking on two Autobots.

'Fall back!' he yells at his squad. 'It's Prime we want, anyway…'

As Fanzone and his officers withdraw from the scene, Bumblebee acknowledges his fellow Autobot.

'Nice moves, Prowl. But I had it under control.'

Before Prowl can respond, there's a loud rumbling.

'This building is fit to collapse,' frowns Prowl. 'Your unruly skirmish has weakened its unstable structure. We need to move out – fast.'

You dash for the main exit. But as you approach, a section of ceiling above it caves in, blocking it completely.

'Maybe I can cut a hole through with my stingers?' suggests Bumblebee.

To try Bumblebee's plan, turn to 67.

To search for another way out, turn to 2.

As you leave the lounge area, you are accosted by a catering 'bot – a walking, talking vending machine.

'Hi there! I'm Tallulah, your Silver Servo buddy for today!' The 'bot's mechanical smile is a bit creepy. 'What can I get you folks?'

Her transparent body displays a range of snacks. You're very hungry. You ask for a chocolate nutri-bar.

'Coming right up! I'll just scan for ID to add that to your account…'

There's a momentary pause, then Tallulah continues, still beaming.

'Sorry folks, but my scans show your presence to be unauthorised. I have summoned my security colleagues.'

Even as she speaks, two guard-bots come rushing into the lounge to join her.

'In the event of your attempting to escape, it will be necessary for my colleagues to render you unconscious with their stun-guns.' Tallulah's smile remains fixed. 'Silver Servo apologise in advance for any inconvenience this may cause.'

To give an excuse for your presence, turn to 25.
To try to make a run for it, turn to 42.

The tracker signal leads you out of the city. Only after a drive of several kilometres does Bumblebee pull up, let you out of his passenger door, and change back into robot mode.

You're in the middle of nowhere. The only feature in an otherwise empty landscape is a large silver box at the side of the road, around which the other Autobots and Sari are gathered.

'It doesn't make any sense,' Prime is saying, as you approach. 'We're right on top of the signal. But the impostor can't be in there!'

'Still – no harm in having a peek,' says Bulkhead. He grasps the box's heavy outer casing and effortlessly wrenches it away – to reveal a complex electronic console.

'Where's Ratchet when you need him?' mumbles Prime.

'I'll just press the lot, shall I, boss?' asks Bulkhead. He brings his heavy fist down on the console.

Instantly, the section of road on which you and your companions are standing – big enough to hold several large vehicles – begins to sink into the ground. You find yourself descending a sheer-walled shaft.

A hundred metres down, the platform slows to a standstill. There is a large opening in the side of the shaft. It leads you into a huge, brightly-lit cavern.

Two large passageways leave the cavern. The one in the far wall has a monorail running through it. A freight vehicle is perched on its single track, being loaded with white cargo containers by a team of worker-bots.

'I've heard about this!' squeals Sari. 'It's a massive underground warehouse! *HomeTech* store their finished 'bots here. They've got this groovy state-of-the-art underground delivery system – all fully automated, with robo-freighters zipping along their own network of tunnels.'

To take a closer look at the cargo containers, turn to 61.
To explore the other passageway, turn to 37.

You find Sari in an annexe to the main packing area, where she's watching the endless stream of Pixie-6 'bots be encapsulated, one at a time, in their transparent packaging pods.

'Great, isn't it?' she enthuses, as a team of worker-bots first vacuum-wrap, then encase each shiny new Pixie-6. ''Bots packing 'bots – and they never get bored or tired!'

Prime joins you in the annex. As he approaches, you're struck by the angry look on his face.

An instant later, both you and Sari find yourselves clasped in Prime's massive metal hands. And his crushing grip is much too tight for comfort.

'Keep still and be silent!' snarls the giant robot. 'Unless you want to find out whether these primitive devices can package humans!'

The unfamiliar voice and cruel eyes are enough to tell you, beyond a doubt, that this isn't the real Optimus Prime…

To do as Prime's impostor says, turn to 46.
To yell for help, turn to 31.

Your attack only fuels Blitzwing's rage.

'You will inconvenience me no longer, pestilent humans!' he rants, preparing for a final, lethal strike.

Suddenly, he is encapsulated by a shimmering force-field. His eyes flash with anger as he is lifted from the floor.

'Thought it was time I joined the party,' growls a familiar voice behind you.

It's Ratchet. He is projecting the magnetic field from his wrists. With a grunt of exertion, he heaves it to one side, flinging Blitzwing against the front ranks of advancing Pixie-6s. The impact sends the domestic 'bots toppling like dominoes, and leaves Blitzwing momentarily dazed.

Drained, but determined, Ratchet quickly conjures another field around the control sphere above, and brings it down to hover beside Sari.

A livid Blitzwing has now regained his feet. Flames blaze around his forearms as he prepares to retaliate.

'Sari!' yells Ratchet. 'The Key!'

Sari grabs the device around her neck, and thrusts its tip into an opening in the control sphere's surface. As she does so, Blitzwing clutches his metal head and gives an agonised scream.

A look of concentration fills Sari's face. The Pixie-6 'bots suddenly come to a halt. As one, they turn to face the howling Decepticon. You realise that it is Sari, not Blitzwing, who is now controlling them.

Each home-helpbot launches a spray of white foam – domestic fire retardant – at the giant Decepticon. Within seconds, Blitzwing is thickly coated in the clinging stuff – blinded, and hardly able to move.

At Sari's command, the Pixie-6s charge headlong at Blitzwing. The tide of 'bots overwhelms him. As he topples to the floor, thousands of Pixie-6s swarm over his massive metal body.

With the Decepticon no longer a threat, your thoughts turn to your fallen comrade. As you, Sari and Ratchet rush to check on Prime, the other three Autobots burst on to the scene, and hurry to join you.

To your relief, Prime is OK. With his friends' help, his gets to his feet. Seeing his Decepticon enemy helplessly pinned down by his former instruments of destruction, he turns to you and Sari.

'I owe you both my thanks. With Blitzwing's plot exposed – and foiled – I shall be able to clear my name. My friends and I will no longer be fugitives.'

'And anytime the boss gets himself on the wrong side of the law again,' adds Bulkhead, with a robotic wink, 'Well – we'll know who to call…'

THE END

Close inspection of the breached wall reveals a sliver of grey metal embedded in it. As the light catches the metal splinter, its surface shimmers with rainbow colours.

You show it to Sari, who raises her eyebrows.

'Looks like Cyberium steel – the stuff a lot of the Autobots' parts are made from. Hold on to it. It's the sort of evidence I think Optimus –'

She breaks off at the sound of footsteps. You both quickly duck behind one of the beam-grille generators.

A group of *HomeTech* scientists are coming along the corridor, lost in conversation.

'We might be able to get out through the hole before they see us!' hisses Sari. 'There's a chance the beams are just data-wipers – to prevent anyone taking restricted info out of the lab. On the other hand, if they are stun beams…'

To stay put, and hope the scientists won't notice you, turn to 9.

To take your chances with the beam-grille, turn to 42.

'It's like kung fu for robots,' explains Sari. 'Prowl studied it back on Cybertron, I think.'

Prowl continues to sit silently. Sari looks restless.

'Look, I'm going to check if the coast is clear. You keep Mister Meditation hcrc company.'

She hasn't been gone long when the massive red and white 'bot you met earlier – Ratchet – comes lumbering towards you.

'Sari's safe with Prime,' he informs you gruffly. 'We've shaken off the cops, so we're heading back to HQ. You better wake up young ninja-bot. There's a demolition robo-crew outside all set to start levelling this place. We need to move out – now.'

Prowl opens one eye disdainfully. 'I'm not sleeping, I'm –'

He is cut off by a mighty crash. A massive plasma-charged wrecking-ball bursts through the wall ten metres away. The building shudders, and a large section of the ceiling collapses, blocking your obvious exit route.

The wall nearest you cracks as another wrecking-ball thumps into it. The ball's next blow turns the cracks into a gaping hole.

'We could get out through there!' yells Prowl. 'But we'll have to time it right!'

To follow Prowl's lead, turn to 67.

To try to find another exit, turn to 2.

You sneak along the right-hand corridor, into the heart of the *HomeTech* lab.

'The news bulletin said the break-in had something to do with these brand new helpbots they're about to release,' whispers Sari. 'So keep your eyes peeled for anything Pixie-6 related.'

You reach an intersection with another corridor. As you go to continue straight on, a wall of translucent pink light – some sort of force-field – suddenly flares into life immediately ahead of you. A slim panel bearing a domed sensor slides from one wall, and a synthetic voice fills the corridor:

'Access to Sector E5 requires Level 8 clearance. Please present pass-chip to proceed.'

'Rats!' hisses Sari. 'I guess we'd better try the other corridors. Let's split up, check out one each, then meet back here. Unless…'

She looks down thoughtfully at the device around her neck.

'I guess there's a slim chance my Key might work as a pass-chip…'

To split up to check out the corridors, turn to 87.

To try Sari's Key, turn to 71.

Sari puffs out her cheeks.

'It's all a bit crazy. This guy insists that Optimus broke into this place last night. He says the cops think that Optimus has been hired by another company to mess things up for *HomeTech* – that's why they're after him.'

She looks thoughtful.

'I remember Dad saying that *HomeTech* are about to launch this cool new domestic 'bot – the Pixie-6 – and that it's a really big deal. So I guess someone might try to sabotage the project. But not Optimus! It must have been someone pretending to be him…'

The Autobots finish questioning the security guard. Bulkhead quickly changes form, morphing into a SWAT-type assault vehicle. Prowl shepherds the guard through Bulkhead's heavy rear doors. He is clearly going to be kept out of the way for a while.

'I'll run some scans around the site's perimeter,' grunts Ratchet. 'See if there's any clue as to who our mystery intruder might have been.'

The veteran Autobot changes into his alternate mode – a medical response vehicle – and pulls away purposefully.

'That leaves inside,' says Prime. 'For which,

thanks to our obliging guard, we have a key…' He holds up a black pass-chip, which looks tiny in his massive metal fingers.

Moving to the wall of the *HomeTech* building, Prime stoops to swipe the chip across a domed sensor. A section of the wall recedes, then slides silently to one side, providing access to a corridor within.

Prime turns to you and Sari.

'Prowl, Bumblebee and I are rather too large to go snooping around in there. Think you can handle it?'

To enter the *HomeTech* building, turn to 91.
To let Sari lead the way, turn to 33.

The Key won't cooperate. Try as she might, Sari cannot get it to repeat its attack on the Pixie-6s.

'Prime, my friend!' yells Blitzwing mockingly. 'Your friends need emergency assistance! Isn't that your thing?'

Prime turns.

'Of course,' continues Blitzwing, 'when I programmed the holotech device to impersonate you, I made sure to include your vehicle form, too.'

He swiftly changes into an exact duplicate of Prime's fire truck alt mode.

'Though why on Cybertron you'd want to be something this dull, I can't imagine.'

Without warning, he races straight at Prime, ploughing into him at full speed. The Autobot topples and hits the floor heavily. He doesn't get up.

Blitzwing quickly morphs back into robot form, grinning.

'Oh dear,' he sneers, advancing on you and Sari once more. 'Your Autobot friend seems to be feeling a little run down!'

To run for it, turn to 41.

To try to revive Prime, turn to 15.

Blitzwing draws nearer, swinging his ice-spiked fists menacingly. A thick coating of ice has materialised over his entire upper body, like a layer of transparent armour.

As the Decepticon approaches, Prime pulls away a large section of his chest-casing – his alt mode windscreen – and brandishes it like a shield.

Blitzwing fixes his Autobot foe with a frosty stare.

'Prepare to be knocked out,' he snarls. 'Cold.'

Lunging at Prime, he unleashes a vicious right hook. Prime quickly swings his shield up to deflect the blow, and follows through with a fierce punch of his own. Blitzwing reels backwards, clutching his jaw.

'You might want some ice on that,' taunts Prime.

Enraged, the Decepticon hurls himself at Prime, only to be sent skidding across the floor on his metal backside by a hefty clout from the Autobot's shield.

To launch a follow-up attack while Blitzwing is down, turn to 48.

To grab your chance to get clear, turn to 8.

Sari stoops to examine something on the floor – a small pool of glistening orange fluid.

'I've seen Bumblebee top up with this stuff,' says Sari. 'It's Cyberium 'bot-oil. Our intruder must have done himself some damage when he smashed through – he sprang a leak!'

She studies the spilt 'bot-oil more closely.

'Once this stuff's been round a 'bot's system, it picks up identity-unique program-code traces. It's kinda like a blood sample. Good evidence – if we had something to scoop it up with…'

A doorway a little further along the corridor leads into a small office – where you find a magna-clip tray and spatula-like ruler perfect for the job.

You're nearly done scraping up the orange gloop when a sound sets your pulse racing. A pair of *HomeTech* guard-bots are patrolling the corridor.

To slip back into the office and hide behind the desk, turn to 9.

To try to think of a better hiding place, turn to 25.

It isn't long before you're wishing you'd stuck with Sari. As you explore alone, you come to an area bustling with police officers. You duck into an alcove before they notice you, then cautiously peer out.

The officers are examining a large doorway. Its heavy sliding doors are badly damaged, their joining edges bent back so that the doors no longer block the opening. They have clearly been wrenched apart with formidable force.

There's a sign beside the doorway:

PIXIE-6 CONTROL SYSTEMS DEVELOPMENT
LEVEL 9 PERSONNEL ONLY

Judging by the police interest, you guess that the mangled doors are the work of last night's intruder. You wonder what lies beyond them to merit a break-in.

Moments later, you get your opportunity to find out – the police officers, having completed their examination, are leaving the area.

To sneak through the damaged doors, turn to 66.
To wait a bit, in case the police return, turn to 70.

A seat belt curls round your waist, and Bumblebee gives a gleeful whoop.

'Time to shake a servo!'

With a roar of engines, both he and Prime tear away. The oncoming police vehicles fall into pursuit.

After a hair-raising chase across the city, you enter the area that Prime mentioned. Scheduled for demolition, its buildings are eerily deserted.

'Split up!' yells Prime.

Bumblebee swerves down a side street. Up ahead is the entrance to a derelict shopping mall. He rattles up the mall's steps and through its smashed doors. As he screeches to a halt, you find yourself being gently ejected from his passenger seat on to the mall floor. By the time you've got to your feet, Bumblebee has changed into robot form.

All three of you hurry into the shadows of the nearest retail unit, and wait to see if you've shaken off the police.

Minutes pass. Then you hear the faint whirr of a motor. A lone police copter-bot is searching the mall.

'I could zap it with my stingers,' whispers Bumblebee, 'but that'll tell the whole force we're here…'

Suddenly, the hovering robot is encapsulated in a shimmering field of energy. It comes to a halt, and begins to twirl round, confused.

A giant red and white robot – almost as big as Prime, but much worse for wear – stomps forward from the other side of the mall. The energy field is coming from twin magnetic generators on his thick mechanical wrists.

'That should stop it transmitting,' grunts the stranger.

'Nice going, old timer!' says Bumblebee. Seeing the scowl on the other robot's grizzled face, he hastily adds. 'Er… I mean… Ratchet…'

You hear the sound of sirens outside.

'Hmph. Sounds like we've got company anyway,' growls Ratchet. 'You'd better get those young organics out of harm's way. I'll distract the cops.'

Bumblebee gestures to a pair of out of service escalators nearby.

'What do you reckon, guys – up or down?'

To scramble up the escalator to the next level of the mall, turn to 3.

To go down a level, turn to 55.

Prime gestures to the tiny cam-bot.

'Does that thing have a data-port, Prowl?'

Prowl gives it a good look over with his microscopic vision, then nods.

'If I can tap into its network,' explains Prime, 'I might be able to access the video feeds from all the other cam-bots working on the same system.

He takes the cam-bot, and carefully inserts his finger-probe into its data-port.

'I should get a quick visual overview of the whole facility – and maybe a fix on our villain…'

For a few seconds, his eyes glaze over with a silver sheen. Then he's back.

'Negative. It worked, but there's no sign of our impostor. We'll just have to track him down ourselves.'

You set off along the passageway, following it until it branches into two.

'What now?' says Bumblebee. 'Left, right – or split up?'

To separate into two parties, turn to 36.

To stick together, and choose a passageway, turn to 72.

Prime responds to your warning – just as Blitzwing's fighter jet unleashes a missile straight at him. With a squeal of skidding tyres, Prime manages to dodge out of its path. The missile rockets past to hit the wall behind you.

The explosion is powerful enough to bring down a whole section of wall and ceiling – right on top of Prime. As the fire truck is crushed below an avalanche of debris, you only escape being squashed flat thanks to its tough Cyberium steel cab.

As the dust settles, you and Sari crawl out from Prime's damaged cab. The dazed Autobot makes a feeble attempt to change. He slowly regains robot shape under the pile of crushing rubble, only to lie motionless beneath it.

Blitzwing converts back from jet form to robot mode, and advances menacingly.

To try to revive Prime, turn to 15.

To hurl rubble at Blitzwing to fend him off, turn to 79.

You find nothing inside the *HomeTech* building to identify the previous night's intruder – until you come to a light, spacious lounge area. It looks like this is where staff members have their coffee breaks.

But at present, it is a scene of devastation. The large section missing from the lounge's transparent ceiling is scattered in fragments across the floor. Several tables below the jagged hole are crushed or buckled.

Clearly, something big and heavy has recently smashed through the polyglaz ceiling.

'Must be where whoever-it-was got in,' says Sari. 'Certainly looks like the work of someone about Prime's size…'

There's a coloured smear on one of the tables. Whoever dropped in landed heavily enough to scratch their paintwork.

Sari scrapes a few paint flakes from the table and wraps them in a napkin from the robo-service counter.

'Evidence!' she says, with a wink.

To continue searching the building, turn to 76.
To head back outside, turn to 12.

As you attempt to get up, you feel suddenly woozy, and black out.

When you come round, it is to find the grizzled face of a huge red and white robot scowling down at you.

'Hmph!' grunts the stranger, straightening. He's almost as tall as Prime, but heavier, and much worse for wear. 'Bit fragile, these organics.'

Someone else leans in – a small girl with bright red hair, in bunches.

'Don't mind Ratchet,' she grins. 'He's always this grumpy. But he's an excellent doc-bot – how do you feel now?'

In fact, you feel much better. You sit up, and look around – to find that your surroundings have completely changed. You're now in a large warehouse-like building, crammed with row upon row of identical robots, all currently inactive.

'I'm Sari,' continues the girl. 'Optimus told us to keep an eye on you. He's gone to see what he can find out about why the police are after him.'

'So once his back was turned,' grunts Ratchet, 'young missy here insists that we drag you along on this ill-advised mission of hers…'

Sari gives him a withering look, then explains.

'This place is where the police recharge their surveillance 'bots. I thought that if we snuck in and scanned their memory banks while they're out of operation, we might pick up some info about why Optimus is in trouble.'

Her face falls a little.

'But we haven't found anything. We were about to leave when you came round.'

Bumblebee sticks his head round a nearby doorway.

'Me and Prowl have found another bunch of 'bots through here,' he says cheerfully. 'We'll check them out, then meet you back at base.'

To go with Sari and Ratchet, turn to 69.

To stay with Bumblebee and Prowl, turn to 20.